Profits

Away somewhere, far off, several business leaders hold a
meeting. It is a swank, upper-level office, in the middle of
Manhattan. The head CEO, a young man with a crew cut, moves
about excitedly in the front. He is dressed in a suave three-piece
suit, with black Italian shoes. The rest of the company looks on,
some elderly men visibly bored, and a few middle-aged women
listening intently, perhaps eyeing up their prospects for a
promotion. "And, as you can see here, the dividends for the
fourth quarter have slightly..." but he is abruptly cut off as the
building violently shakes. He ceases directing attention to the
keynotes of his Powerpoint presentation as he tumbles to the
ground. Everyone screams and the room falls into a panic. As
dust clouds kick up it is clear that the building is crumbling. A
portly gentleman with greying hair, mocha skin, and a powder
blue shirt runs for the door but the floor falls out from
underneath him. All of the employees tumble into the ocean.
Emerging from the ashes of this rubble, a gargantuan
beast rises up in the middle of the city. It is a perplexing and
awe-inspiring sight; it appears to be a seven-hundred-foot tall
venture capitalist. Though it is comprised of the writhing bodies
of many of its former employees, it forms a cohesive whole.
Outstretching its arm which is clothed in a single-breasted suit, it
roars and yet assumes a recognizable human form. It stands up,
blocking the path of the sun, its tie taking form. Many people on
the street simply stop and stare in befuddled wonder and horror.
"Hello, everyone," its bellows in a clear and authoritative voice,
"I do apologize for disturbing everyone with that. As for the
sunlight, I feel for too long it has been offered in a substandard
version for free. If you'd like to get a better quality version of
sunlight, I offer a premium discount at only twelve dollars a
month." Its words sound reassuring and it flashes a cajoling
smile as it bends down to get a look at its clients. Its chin barely
scrapes the ground and its head sits right next to a skyscraper,

almost dwarfing the bottom of it. A teenager with a shopping bag in her hand, headphones around her ears, a fedora, and a red sundress, simply stares into its face, which now that it's closer, she can tell is made up of hundreds of wriggling accountants.

The corporation now crosses lands, stretches across states, puts out its foot and leaps over the ocean to jump through countries, hops from continent to continent. It motivates stockholders in several Midwestern states for money to invest in. Along the way as it lands on the ground it tears up the gravel and shreds a few bushes. "Such is the cost of business," it mutters to itself. When trees are in its path it knocks them out the way. With over a million dollars stuffed in its pockets it heads to Thailand to check on its factories.

When it peers through the window it sees a few children look tired as they hunch over their knitting table. The owner of this place, a pudgy man with balding hair, a thick black mustache, a tank top that barely holds in his raging gut, and messy khaki pants, stops to yell at them. The corporation removes the roof and steps inside. "Oh...oh my..." the owner staggers.

"Don't worry, there's no reason to be alarmed," the corporation comforts him. Turning towards the kids, he commands, "Let's quit slacking off and get back to work. You all get paid a good ten cents an hour and I won't allow riding the clock on my watch." He taps one small boy who is dozing off on the shoulder and makes a sewing motion to motivate him. The room resumes its usual bustle as the corporation backs out, returns the roof to the building, and continues on its way.

Coming to a busy intersection, the corporation ignores all the confused and astonished drivers, who gasp at its astonishing size as they sit in their cars, and gingerly tiptoes across the highway (so as not to stomp on and crush any vehicles), approaching a small strip mall. This one is less frequented, being on the outskirts of town. The corporation kneels down as it approaches the parking lot, taking note of the SUVs parked here, the tiny shops, the translucent windows, and how a few workers are out on their smoke breaks. It lightly taps on the door of an Asian take-out service.

"Yes?" the woman at the counter asks. As she comes to the front she witnesses the corporation and is horrified.

"Hi," it begins in an apologetic tone, "I really hate to have to tell you this, but we've decided that this area is very nice to do business in, and unfortunately we've chosen to set up shop here." The woman takes a step back and still can't seem to register what is going on. The corporation chuckles, then continues, "What that means is, you'll have to move your business." It offers a conciliatory grin as it says this, flashing its wide teeth, with traces of legs and arms within it.

"But I can't do that!" the woman begins protesting. "This is my place of business! I make money here!"

The corporation grabs the roof of the restaurant in its left hand and lifts it off its foundations. Dust and debris drop from its edges as the employees cling to any surface they can to avoid plummeting to the ground. "Thank you for your understanding," the corporation soothes them as its places them aside and steps into the now vacated spot.

Turning a corner, the corporation is coming around to see how one of its local chapters is doing. It scuffles along, buds of itself asexually falling off its arm as it moves. Bosses and secretaries scramble to stand up and move around after they have been dropped to the ground. It comes to a dark brown building whose windows let in a bit of sunlight. Outside the building a worker has others gathered around. As he puffs away on a cigarette he vents his frustrations. "Well, you know, I'm just sayin', lately they've been making us come in on weekends, and a lot of us still aren't getting raises even though we've done twice the usual work lately..."

The corporation stands a foot away and observes this guy. His thick, straight hair stands parted on his head. He has dark, almost seemingly bruised features, with some slight stubble creeping onto his face. He holds his cigarette in between his middle and index fingers tightly, his arms making wide and sweeping motions as he talks. His sleeves are rolled up to the elbows, revealing a dearth of hair on his arms. A few of his co-workers nod as if to agree. The rest just listen to his harangue. "I mean, I don't know, maybe we should form a union or something..."

Everyone else gasps at this assertion. "Mark, do you know what the bosses would say if they heard you talk like that?" an older woman interjects, bespeckled with frizzy hair and a few moles on her arm.

"But that's it," he lectures, seeming to gain steam with his anger, "that's what they'll do to us if we let this go on. Look, let's just go back to work and we'll talk about this later..."

This is more than the corporation can bear. It comes jogging to where the workers are gathered. When they spot him charging ear a few back up. Two even run into the building. Mark stands his ground as the others near him slightly cower. "Hey, Marky," it addresses him in a familiar tone, "I heard what you were saying. And we don't need that negative attitude in the workplace."

Mark throws down his cigarette and points. "And just who do you think you are?" he snarls.

"Why, I'm the corporation. I created this place that employs you and signs your checks. And I'll have you know," the bass of its voice drops, "I don't appreciate your tone. You're inciting hostility with our company."

Mark's eyes squint and he runs his hands through his hair. "Well, what do you expect? I'm always having extra projects thrown at me, I don't see my wife and kids as much anymore, and on top of that, the boss here is breathing down my neck! Are you going to do something about it?" Mark's face is now red.

"I'll look into it," the corporation says, before slowly reaching out and hoisting Mark up. His squeals are silenced as the corporation places a hand over Mark's mouth. "Can anyone tell me what position Mark held at this office?" it asks everyone else in a gentle tone.

Though the group is initially too frightened to answer, one man, who looks to be balding and sports a ragged red beard, replies, "He's the assistant creative director."

The corporation stands tall in front of them, choosing its next directive carefully. "Well, his spot is now vacant, if anyone is interested in filling it." It whistles as it strolls off, slinging Mark over its shoulder. Many of its employees on its back struggle to muffle Mark's screams for help. "Don't worry, we're directing you to our human resources department," a lady trapped him reassures Mark.

Peering over the roof at the United States Capitol, which has been temporarily taken off to allow it to meet at this hearing, the corporation looks in. Hundreds of press helicopters fly around it and capture video of the senators below. In turn, they stare up at the sky, some annoyed with the widespread coverage of this event, some befuddled by the corporation's gargantuan mass, some eager to discuss matters with it, and others frustrated by its mere appearance here.

"Gentlemen, gentlemen, let's call this hearing of Congress to a beginning," the vice president stands and announces. The black suit he wears gives him a lean appearance, though his figure could already best be described as lanky. He has a red handkerchief tucked away in his breast pocket, in what some consider a dapper twist. The noise begins to die down now that the vice president has risen and begins a formal statement.

"Now that I have everyone's attention, I would like to welcome the corporation to our chambers. Though it was a controversial move to grant him free speech, the measure has gone through. Some may disagree with the ruling but so it stands."

The corporation straightens its tie, a few employees cascading down its calf as a result, and waves at the helicopters swaying by, as well as at the massive audience of onlookers gathered nearby. "Citizens of the United States of America, I'd like to take this opportunity to greet you all. As many of you are familiar with my products and generosity, no doubt you will join me in celebrating this glorious triumph of liberty."

A junior member of Congress, a young looking man with blond hair, a strong jaw, and who was just sipping on a cup of water, slams his fist on his desk. "This isn't freedom! This means you'll just buy your way into influence!" he shouts, his voice sounding hoarse. A few of his colleagues restrain him in his seat as he starts to jerk up.

The corporation places its finger to its chin, then steps back with its left foot. "This is the same sort of anti-deregulation rhetoric we've been hearing for years. People," the corporation fling sits arm to its side to indicate an air of openness, "America is all about freedom. Are you going to let the government clamp down on our right to do business and make a profit? Will you let them take away your freedom as consumers?"

At its feet, the nearby group of onlookers stir. Some cheer at its impassioned speech and wave banners declaring their support for the corporation, others mutter amongst themselves how it's far too big. The vice president stands once again. "No matter what one's opinion is on this matter, we must respect the vote placed today and honor the corporation's right to free speech."

The corporation and others applaud at this declaration. Reaching up, the vice president and the corporation shake hands. "After you're wrapped up with this we have a seat on our shareholders' committee for you," the corporation whispers into the vice president's ear.

Several waves rollick to the coast as the corporation swims in the ocean. It is enjoying itself, doing languid backstrokes, starting up into the sun with relaxed and vacant eyes, its feet, covered in dress shoes, rising to the surface. First it ducks underwater and plumbs the depth of the sea. It inspects all that is on the ground below, observes the fish, drifts around, looks at all the rocks embedded in the surface, turns them over, and shakes them to see if anything comes out. While it does so several CEOs and secretaries that make up its forehead scramble to escape to the top, so as to avoid drowning. Having tired of being underneath, the corporation once again swims to the surface. As it arises in the water it takes on a truly mythic nature, as only its knees reach the massive ocean. Once the sun hits its skin that's when it begins to shine as it brushes its clothes in an attempt to dry off.

Outstretching its arms, the corporation yawns, admiring how this beautiful blue hue seems to stretch for miles. The corporation now feels an urge stab at itself. Bracing back its shoulder blades, it reaches down and unzips its pants. What follows is a stream of urine which pours into the water. As it finishes relieving itself the corporation lets out a deep sigh of satisfaction. Adjusting its pants, it sloshes its legs through the ocean, seeking to explore this myriad environment. It wonders if there's been any excavation of this area for untapped natural resources.

As it continues walking it feels a deep groan in its stomach. Doubling over, it feels nauseous. After all, it reasons to itself, it does carry a lot of people. As it stands back up, it goes right back to the doubled-over position, vomiting in the process. Thousands of liters of garbage and waste create splashes as they are dumped near the fishes and sharks.

Once it turns around, though, it finds a group of vacationing beachgoers surveying its every action. Behind them stands a tall, shiny hotel. One of the swimmers who has damp and curly hair points at the corporation. "Oh my god! What the hell! You can't do that!" The rest of the group rush to the shore where the waves lap at their feet. They threaten the corporation with claims they have observed all its transgressions and will report them.

The corporation makes its way towards them, taking care not to move too fast so that a tsunami is not created. "Whoa,

whoa, guys, let's not panic. What you saw here was an accident. I apologize for my lack of discretion. I felt sick and had no other choice."

The swimmer who yelled at him fires back, "Yeah but you still can't vomit in the ocean!"

The corporation turns around, grits its teeth, and reaches into its breast pocket for its cell phone. Dialing a number, when it gets an answer it whispers, "Hey. We have a situation on our hands. PR disaster. Hmm? Ye...yeah. Get a clean-up crew here."

Being flanked by dozens of colleagues that grow in number as its existence is popularized (CNN recently did a story on its ever-expanding size; the public was astonished how the corporation became by sheer legal will an actual living breathing person), the corporation strolls into Wall Street, looking around in excitement at all the ebullient activity occurring. Thousands of investors run about, yelling instructions and announcements to one another, with numbers flashing at lightning speed on giant tickers above. It is a conglomeration of sweaty flurry, money being handled, and dumbfounded spectators.

"This is an interesting area, gentlemen. My kind of thing," the corporation comments to his friends. It turns its head to smile at Larry, a financial analyst for a think tank located in Maryland. Larry is balding with short curls dominating only the sides of his head. His face is swollen and slightly pink, giving him a cherubic appearance which seems offbeat with his tweed suits and thick-framed glasses.

As several of his coterie jot down quick findings on their notepads, the corporation braces its knees, balls up its fists, and raises them above its head. "What are you doing?" Freddy, a protege with a beard, asks. The corporation slams both of its massive fists into the wall of this structure. His peers gasp. Activity momentarily halts in this busy sector, which is a rarity for this area.

"Wooo!" the corporation exclaims, flailing as it punches through a bit more concrete and wood. It falls to its side, clumsily stretching its feet out (several people dart out of the way so as not to be hit). Freddy and Larry run up to try and restrain it but are easily swatted away. Scrambling to its feet, the corporation takes a running charge and tackles a few chairs, computers, and some scaffolding on the opposite side.

Blood-curdling shrieks of horror ring out as half of the people there attempt to escape the corporation's path of destruction. A few men, however, calmly walk over to congratulate it. One man, with a side part and bushy eyebrows, pats the corporation on the back. "I like what you're doing here. Really taking charge of this place."

The corporation stands up, being careful not to bump its head on the lighting near the top, and lets out an embarrassed chuckle. "Oh, you know, just day-to-day stuff. I didn't really like the way this place looked. Figured I would switch it up."

The corporation stomps its foot on the ground, creating a minor crater that leaves a bit of dust drifting from the ceiling (even the corporation's newest admirer has to grab a nearby beam to keep from falling) while laughing. Now it wanders over to another corner and pries open the wall with its bare hands, its finger getting a few splinters stuck in them as a result. It persists through the minor aggravation until the barrier has been split. Here lie a few security vaults. It walks in, tearing off the door, and rips out the cord of the shrieking alarm.

Noticing several bundles of cash, the corporation begins pocketing them, stuffing its pants with as much money as it can. This drowns out some of its hip and calf, as they fall out its pants leg and splatter to the floor. Some of the interns comprising its fingernail attempt to touch the money but it just picks them out of its body.

Several people peek inside the massacre and catch the corporation taking this stashed currency. "Hey! That's our money!"

The corporation freezes as a few people, including a woman in a wheelchair and a man wearing a plaid shirt and khaki shorts, point fingers at him.

"You can't take that!" an elderly woman says.

As it deposits a final stack in its back pocket, the corporation explains itself. "Oh, don't worry. I'll be investing this for your own good." It takes a few steps, almost seeming to half-skip its way around the crowd.

"Are you sure?" the woman asks.

"Of course," it announces back as it leaves, "you can trust me. I have this all under control."

Ducking around a hill, the corporation sneaks through the rural terrace. Being early morning, the sun is still coming out, casting a mild afterglow on the landscape. Dew is still fresh on the grass; the branches do not sway with the afternoon breeze. Peering beyond a tree, the corporation locates the approximate address it is looking for. Slowly shuffling so as not to wake the other tenets, it maneuvers around a few cars (so as not to accidentally step on and squash them) and slides up to the door of its intended target. This man lives on the second floor; the banister is of a black steel baroque design, with the doors a drab green, with hints of molding on a few of them.

Sticking out its finger, the corporation gently taps the door a few times. Even it can hear the vibrations this causes. Though it is eager to speak to this worker, it quickly glances around to make sure no one catches it here. After a minute the door opens.

A stocky Hispanic man, with a bushy mustache and wearing a muscle shirt, stands there, rubbing his eyes and still half-awake. "Yes?" he asks in an accent.

"Hi. Emanuel Rodriguez?" the corporation struggles to say quietly.

"Yes," Emanuel responds.

"Hi Emanuel. I hate to bother you but we need a surplus of toys to be shipped, and I'd love it if you could come in for the weekend."

Emanuel leans an arm against the edge of his door and purses his lips. "No way. Today my day off. My little girl and I go out to park today." Even through his rough syntax there is a tone of indignation. Looking past Emanuel, the corporation glimpses a couch, a television set and some clothes thrown about the meager space.

"While I am very sorry to spring this news on you at the last minute, the influx of sales demands that we increase productivity to satisfy customer demand."

As the corporation attempts to peek its head in, Emanuel stands his ground. "No. I don't have protective suit here. As well, I cough lately. I report gas leak but no word come back." His hair is short and faded at the sides.

The corporation rears back and clasps its hands behind its back. "As you've most likely heard from your supervisors, we are working on that gas leak." When the corporation got wind of a leaking valve, it nixed maintenance because that would have cost too much.

"But I have bad asthma now. Very nasty smell in there," Emanuel says.

"Emanuel? Who this?" his wife asks, sauntering to the door. She is dressed in gym shorts, slippers, and a baggy shirt, holding their young daughter in her arms. Her thick black hair is tied back into a ponytail and her hazel eyes suggest a world of yearning.

"Nothing. Work." Emanuel tries to wave her off.

Her mouth opens and she turns to him. "But you say we go to park today!"

Emanuel squints and rubs his forehead. "We will. Let me handle this." She saunters off as Emanuel grunts and rolls his eyes.

"The ol' ball-and-chain, eh?" the corporation jokes, resting its arm on the barricade.

"Yes. Look, I come in, but only for few hours, okay?"

"Sure. We just need you for a bit to operate the conveyor belt."

Emanuel stops. "No. Not there."

The corporation raises an eyebrow. "What? Why not?"

"There rats there. They run everywhere."

The corporation puts its head down, then raises it back up. "Why didn't you say anything?"

"I have. I told boss three times." He holds up three fingers for emphasis.

"Okay. Okay. Look..." the corporation stares out into space, thinking, tapping its foot in the process, "just punch in and unload the freight. We'll have you there until twelve."

"Fine. I get overtime?"

"Sure."

"And are loose bolts fixed on second floor?"

"We got those in earlier in the week." The corporation hasn't ordered them yet.

"Fine. I be there. Let me get dressed."

"Alrighty. We appreciate all your hard work, Emanuel!" The corporation dashes off.

The actors up on stage poise themselves for the coming denouement. All is hushed in this small conservatory; a lone spotlight focuses on the man on stage. He wears a vest, tight jeans, a light beard, and the expression on his face is painful but artificial. A woman in a dress kneels by him, presumably acting out her character. About forty or so audience members fill this tiny space; several cough or silently writhe about in their seat.

Just as the two on stage start to recite their lines, the corporation barges in, unannounced. It has slimmed down in size due to layoffs in its body but still barely manages to squeeze in the door. Everyone is caught slightly off-guard by its appearance. A couple on a date jump as it flings open the door and rushes inside.

"Um, excuse me," one of the actors breaks character, stopping in his tracks.

As the corporation stops before the audience, parts of its chest wriggle free and run through the audience, soft drink bottles in hand. It keeps in mind the roped barrier between the audience and the play, as if to enforce some form of respect.

"Good evening, ladies and gentlemen. I apologize profusely for interrupting this play," the corporation begins, throwing its hands into the air. As it paces around the audience, it narrates, "As this appears to be a mighty fine sense of entertainment going on, we just thought we'd introduce you to our new line of drinks, Energy-X. You've probably been getting thirsty sitting here watching this suspenseful plot unfold. Why not have a gulp of our new product to quench your desire and give you the drive you need?" One of its employees near its forehead shows off a can to demonstrate. "It's infused with guarana to replace that tired, empty feeling."

All throughout the theater, where the lights are dimmed, the brown marble floor was showing some cracks, and a few doorways lined the back of the wall, was a growing sense of grumbling discontent. One of the men in front, a young teenager in a fedora and skinny jeans, says, "We don't appreciate commercialism here. I just want to watch the play."

The corporation slouches against the stage and crosses one leg over the other. "Yes, but how much more exciting would this be after a refreshing taste of this drink?" Several of the corporation's workers momentarily break off and stroll throughout the audience, urging people to take samples.

One elder woman obliges. She smacks her lips and remarks it isn't half-bad.

"Excuse me, sir, but we really are offended you interrupted our performance. Aren't those drinks made with uranium as well?" one of the thespians on stage interrupts.

The corporation turns to him, shielding its eyes from the stage lights with its hand. "Reports that they had a small amount are, in fact, true. But we've since recalled those and our new formula no longer contains uranium." The corporation never did understand why people complained about the uranium, since it thought that's where the unique flavor came from.

"We'll have to ask you to leave. There is absolutely no soliciting in this building," the female actor commands, pointing to the door. Several audience members refuse to taste the drink or even hold the can in their hands.

"This isn't quite soliciting, just more a sample of our product." The corporation takes a gander at the poster for next month's performance. "What if I could promote my drink at a bigger venue? Perhaps, Broadway?" The two actors glance at each other, wondering where it is going with this. "With you two as the leading stars?"

The man takes a few steps forward, his hands in his pockets. The woman slumps against a wall, weighing the decision in her mind. "As a gesture of my appreciation for your craft, why don't you both consider it over a thousand dollars each?" The corporation draws stacks of money out of its pockets. Several audience members are sipping on the carbonated beverage, remarking to one another now how tasty it is. They have been provided glasses with crushed ice to pour them into.

"Okay, fine," the male actor mumbles.

"Great! Continue on. Pretend I'm not even here," the corporation urges them, twirling its finger to signal so, and then sitting on the ground to observe the continuing action.

"Fiona, I never considered.." the male actor resumes before he's cut off.

"Oh, just one more thing," the corporation saunters up, with a can. "If you could just integrate this into the scene," he says, handing it over.

"I really don't drink soda," the male actor says. He bites his lip and holds the can away from him.

"Oh, just pretend. Isn't that what you all do anyway?" The female actor shoots it a glare. "Just incorporate it naturally. I don't want it to seem forced." It now sits back down as one audience member complains of his wife now feeling dizzy.

From the veneer of space the planet Earth appears much different than before. The oceans are still there, the continents still intact, the wispy atmosphere still contained within its own biological sphere. But now the visage of the corporation is noticeable even when compared to the stars and the sun, it having grown to immense size yet again. As it yawns and awakens its sprawling body stretches over half of Earth. It begins in the morning by swimming from continent to continent, seeing how each of its branches are doing. Dotting all of the landscapes are factories and warehouses, thousands of employees running about, writing memos, unloading freight, trading gossip, and brokering deals.

The corporation stares at the sky, where clouds drift with advertisements written into them (the corporation has worked with a team of molecular scientists to configure some aspects of nature so they naturally promote its product). It sees people go by, using its paper, wearing its clothes, talking on its phone, and driving its car. It has swelled in proportion, magnetically attracting various workers as it runs on by, who now live in its forehead, wrist, and chest. They have ceased squirming and instead lay still, some perishing from hunger, which the corporation does not even notice because they are buried so deeply within its body.

"You know," the corporation wonders aloud as it snacks on an ice cream cone, "I never did like the name 'Earth' anyway. Too clangy and short. It will never get across to the customer. I'd like to re-name it something more marketable and catchy. Maybe...like...Life Inc." The corporation nods its head a few consecutive times and claps quickly. "Yeah, that's it. Sums up what we're about with a slight formal twist. Still to-the-point like Earth, though." It uproots a tree, tears away some bark, and quickly carves in its idea as a reminder.

Meanwhile, in outer space, two aliens approach Earth. Their spacecraft is a sleek but sturdy ship that hovers through the vacuum of the universe but intensifies in speed as it descends through the atmosphere. Their bodies are thin and lanky, with hammer-shaped faces, slanted black eyes, and greenish-grey skin. The lights on their control panel blink wildly as they shift their vehicle into landing mode. One of them, Zordok, spins halfway in his swiveling chair. "So you cool with landing on Earth for a quick break?" he asks his friend Mortar.

Mortar returns from unlocking the first door of the vessel and slouches in the seat next to him, devouring a few chips. "Yeah, I guess. I have to take a leak real bad. Plus, haven't seen Earth in a while. Remember that time we chased that guy around for three hours saying we were going to probe him?" he reminisces, bursting into laughter as he does so.

"Yeah," Zordok giggles, and they land on safe terrain.

As they shuffle towards the airlock Mortar stretches and approves, "Ah, man, this trip across galaxies is exactly what we needed. Really good to get away from the empire and the wife for a bit." Mortar walks down the ramp as Zordok turns off the engine.

"Yeah, man, seemed like you were letting the overlord get to you a bit there."

They both pause, sensing something different. "This place look different to you?" Mortar says to Zordok.

Having seen their ship park, the corporation wanders over to them. "Hi. Can I be of some assistance?" he asks them.

"Oh, no, we're fine," Zordok replies, getting an eye at this massive creature, "just stopping for a break."

"This is Earth, correct?" Mortar asks the corporation.

"It was formerly Earth. Welcome now to Life Inc."

"Life...Inc.?" Mortar says.

"Yes. I see you've parked your vehicle over there. If you wouldn't mind moving it over there to that lot..." the corporation points to a parking garage manned by a toll-taker, "that would be fantastic. Now, would you be interested in a single visit or a week-long pass? For this month we've reduced visit prices to the low price of three hundred..."

"Wait, wait, visit price?" Zordok questions him, his eyes blinking, his upper lip rising in the right corner. The grass around them is neatly trimmed to half an inch and several bushes dot the outskirt of the land.

"Of course. We can discuss this if you follow me..." the corporation slightly bows as he sways his arms to the side.

"Eh, no thank you. I think we'll just leave," Zordok refuses as he nudges Mortar to follow him back to the ship.

"Are you sure? We've got some wonderful sights and amazing attractions. The Gulf of Mexico Water Park, the Tibetan Mountain Loop-de-Loop, the Outback Camping Zone..." it attempts to convince them, easily dwarfing their vehicle as it approaches their ship, a visual which several people turn their heads to.

"Nah. Thanks anyway," Mortar says, and they hop back in and fly off.

The corporation watches them take off and grunts.

"Man, what happened to Earth?" Mortar says as he mans the control stick to steer them away.

"I know, it really went to shit, didn't it?" Zordok complains.

"Oh, well, let's fly back home. Maybe we can stop by the Andromeda galaxy later. I hear they've got a good new restaurant there."

"Yeah, let's do that."

They drift through space, careening in darkness, as the corporation walks off and continues issuing instructions.

The Therapist

The therapist skips, jumps, and runs. Hurling himself
over a couch and making a diving tackle for the mail, he looks
through the clutter of envelopes on his floor. He glances eagerly
at the various letters he has been sent. Finally, his eyes light up.
He has found it; his Holy Grail, his balm of Gilead, his panacea.
With eager enthusiasm he announces, "Yes! Yes! I have found it!
Oh, blessed Lord, I have found it!" The therapist holds up an
issue of *Psychology Today*, triumphantly. "Now I can find out
what makes dogs tick, the collective unconscious of the canine
species, if you will." The therapist glances at his dog, which
gives him a frightened and sincere look, its head in its paws on
the floor. "I can understand your cowardice in my presence.
Your mother left you at an early age. Thus, you have a fear of
abandonment, whilst also possessing an undertow of
subservience to authority, mostly paternal figures." The therapist
hops off, confident in its expert analysis of his own pet.

The Therapist In the Grocery Line

The therapist waits a while, with bread, cereal, yogurt,
three beach towels, and a small rodent in his cart. He is now third
in line. The therapist is dressed in a tasteful dark blue suit, brown
oxford shoes, a white shirt with a black tie, his thin gray hair
slicked back while he strokes his wizened beard. With no
warning the therapist jumps on the counter. "I have determined
this line is one giant phallic symbol. If you will notice, it is quite
straight and large, typically the shape of a penis. I believe the
consumer and the supermarket work in synergy and express a
sense of male dominance and aggression. The consumer wishes
to empower himself or herself, subconsciously joining behind
one another to create a sense of shared identity. The supermarket
fulfills its ultimate desire of power by organizing and
legitimizing a line, a sense of order and uniformity. It's really

quite simple if you look at it." Everyone in the line claps. The therapist thanks them and cuts ahead to the front of the line, the total of his goods being forty-three dollars and sixty seven cents. The therapist punches the cashier in the face and walks away.

The Therapist While Mowing the Lawn

The therapist, now wearing a light grey flannel suit with a blue shirt and a dot-patterned silk tie, pushes his lawn mower up and down his front lawn. With a thoughtful pause he mulls over what he is about to say. "To me, mowing the lawn represents a yearning for stability. This preference for upkeep suggests an earlier chaotic home life. A hatred of what one thinks of as 'unsightly' could suggest repressed inner demons. The obsession with appearances in suburbia is an apt metaphor for an attempt to feed on addiction and replace the emptiness within with well-trimmed lawns." During his analysis the therapist has failed to notice he has run over his left foot, which is now bleeding all over the place.

One Therapist Meets Another

"Hello, fellow therapist!"
"Oh, hi! You're a male!"
" Yes, I am! How are you?"
"I'm fine. By the way, your inclusion into my private business is a sign that you are dealing with an internal sense of isolation, possibly because of negligent parents."
"Really now? What would you label this, as a disorder?"
"Hmm. I'd shoot for obsessive-compulsive psychoactive necrophobic type-A hemophiliac narcissist, with a hint of manic-depressive Asperger's."
"You think? I always pegged myself as more antisocial."
"Oh, no. You only display two symptoms of that."

"Interesting. Of course, the fact that you pointed out that I'm a male therapist hints that you have unresolved sexual conflict, such as an Oedipal struggle with the idea of authority stemming from the opposite sex."

"Wow. How long have you practiced that?"

"Three years."

"I'd say you've perfected it."

"Thank you." He checks his watch. "Look at the time. I must be on my way to help a client through their cheese neurosis."

"Understandable. Well, nice meeting you. Have a good day." She waves.

"You too." He waves back. The two therapists merrily stroll towards their separate paths.

The Therapist While Taking a Shit

The therapists' khaki pants are around his ankles. The sleeves of his black suit stretch as he rests his chin upon his fist. As he squints while staring into the distance, he announces to his son who is playing in the hallway, "You know, Kyle, disposing of fecal matter is symbolic of ridding ourselves of unwanted desires. Feces are viewed as disgusting and horrendous, much as the violent impulses of our id are. And yet we must confront them every day. The rectum is the superego, which places societal pressure on us, as opposed to the id. And, in this case, the toilet is the ego, which flushes away the bowels of our id by negotiating with the superego. Confronting one's shadow is necessary to reach a higher self-actualization, hence the sigh after you have used the lavatory. Are you jotting all of this down, Kyle?" His son plays with a toy airplane, making crashing noises as he lands it. "Regressive behavior to avoid dealing with difficult situations. Understandable as a coping mechanism." The therapist flushes the toilet.

The Therapists' Annual Convention

In a civic center, about five hundred or so therapists have gathered in the meeting room, all sitting in folding chairs. The stench of cigarette smoke on some jackets can be smelled, accompanied by the cacophony of their own individual conversations. The head therapist takes the podium, clears his throat, and holds up his hand to gain control and silence. "Okay, everyone, let's get started. We have a lot to get to during this particular gathering. First of all, I have to say I'm very proud of the microphones at this podium. They're more phallic-shaped than ever. Good job, guys. Now, one issue a lot of you have been wondering about is the goal we're ultimately trying to reach with therapy. What should we call it?"

"Self-actualization?" one therapist yells out.

"Good try but you know our guidelines: you must raise your hand to make a suggestion." He picks out one who does such.

"Self-realization?"

"Too stark."

"Self-awakening?"

"Strikes too much of religion."

"Self-growth?"

"Perfect! Just enough ambiguity to slide by, while leaving the door open for infinite sessions. Now..." he consults the outline he has brought with him, "have we decided whether the mother figure is domineering or passive?"

One therapist stands up. "By a majority vote of two hundred and thirty to one hundred and two we have decided the mother is a passive and beneficial archetype."

"Glad that's cleared up. Any other questions or concerns?"

"Yes." One of them stands up. "Are we Jungians or behaviorists?"

"Behaviorists with a slight archetypal bent." The head therapist pauses to see someone in the back now stand up with his hand raised, an urgent look on his face. "Yes, you?"

"Uh, yeah, a few days ago a patient of mine brought this up. What's the official meaning of a dolphin wearing a bowler hat in a dream?"

"Ah, never encountered that one before. I'm leaning towards hatred of the self. Anyone else?"

"I'd suggest the idea that the client is anxious about the future."

"That's a decent explanation. We might go with that."

"If I can say something, may I suggest that it represents conflicting emotions about a lost loved one?"

"Well done. Just broad enough to encompass a good range of experiences. Alright, well that concludes the annual therapists' convention. Help yourself to drinks and food on the way out, but remember if you take too many your greed is really just compensating for your inferiority complex."

The Therapist While Having Sex With His Wife

The therapist is thrusting into his wife, back and forth, up and down, the sweat slightly drenching his red shirt and brown tweed jacket. "I believe the reason I am interested in you is because you remind me of my sister. It implies enough incestuous urges to arouse mild interest. Your slender features and broad nose are exactly like hers, as well as your preference for sweetening your tea. The fact that you're a Democrat and she's a Republican is irrelevant. When I look at you sometimes I see her."

His wife sighs, visibly frustrated and not turned on one bit. "You don't even know my favorite color, do you?"

"Why? Is it yellow? Because if it is yellow, that represents an optimistic disposition and an outgoing, extroverted personality. Of course, yellow can also symbolize anxiety and sickness. The color yellow is known to make small babies agitated."

His wife throws him off her, gets up, and goes to the bathroom.

The Therapist's Solution To the Problem of War

A young man, in his mid-twenties, lies on the therapist's' couch. The therapist's jacket is off and the sleeves of his black dress shirt are rolled up. "War is the release of contained sexual frustration within a society. Dormant limbo is expressed via ritualized violence. We vent our fears and hatreds onto the enemy of the current moment. My way to stop it, you ask? I say we place all of the world leaders on medication. My dosage for our current President would begin with a small bit of lithium, then move up to Paxil and from there we could see about heroin and cocaine..."

"Aren't heroin and crack illegal?"

"Oh, that is true. Well, we'll find prescriptions for whatever drugs are legal now."

"But what about just talking through the problems?"

The therapist laughs. "Why would you do that? Medicating people is a much more quick and efficient way of dealing with problems."

What Does the Therapist Think Of This Story?

The therapist sits at his mahogany oak desk, quite shiny and nicely polished, with a globe on one corner and a full bookshelf behind him. This time the therapist wears a grey suit and green shirt with a black tie. He stares at you, the reader. "Well, for one, I feel the author has a gross misunderstanding of psychology. His references to pseudo-Freudian theories are intended to compensate for what he may feel is his intellectual inferiority. Also, much of modern psychology is actually rooted in a cognitive and scientific approach. By reducing me to a stereotype, I become easier to criticize." He takes a sip of water from a mug. "In addition, he has unresolved stress issues, which manifest themselves in the form of this acidic satire. Clearly his mistrust of the psychiatric field signals a lack of respect for authority, which is one of the hallmarks of antisocial personality disorder." The therapist leans back in his chair. Several diplomas can be seen on his wall. "His lack of complete development for any of the characters you have seen thus far reveals his narrow black-and-white view of the world, which falls under the jurisdiction of borderline personality disorder, as well as a refusal to truly empathize with others, a condition we label narcissistic." The therapist checks his watch. "Many writers have suffered from bipolar disorder and the author here may be no different. Oh sure, he can comment on our culture's lack of self-reliance or how 'therapy' may truly fail to solve problems because it risks being self-indulgent. He may even raise the issue that psychology now pushes medication to both pacify the public and because pharmaceutical companies have a hand in such matters." The therapist clears his throat. "Above all, I truly think the core issue with this story is...I'm sorry, it appears we've run out of time. We'll have to continue this session next week. Thank you."

The Chicken Crossed the Road

The chicken crossed the road. We distinctly remember
that. When we asked him why, he claimed it was to get to the
other side. We highly doubt this, because for one nobody crossed
a road just to get to the other side. Perhaps he was going
somewhere, and had to cross the road out of necessity, but we are
skeptical about it being a mere whim. Edward said why can't the
chicken just cross the road of his own volition, he can talk after
all, why not just go around crossing roads of his own free will,
but we all told Edward to shut up, he gets annoying sometimes.
Thomas doubts the chicken crossing the road, rather he believes
the road crossed the chicken, though we contemplated this, we
denied its validity, we saw the chicken in motion, not the road.
Thomas countered that how do we really know we really saw it
was the chicken who initiated movement? Interesting, Thomas,
we said, but even the chicken himself admits it was he who
crossed the road. Gary believes the chicken was dodging an
oncoming vehicle, they're a bit smarter than armadillos, though
Gary sometimes thinks armadillos are depressed and suicidal.
Not so, Gary, we said, because if the chicken was worried about
being run over he wouldn't be in the road in the first place. Gary
pointed out that maybe the chicken didn't foresee a car in the
road, that sometimes you can get stuck in those types of
situations. We've never been in that situation, we reminded
Gary, and besides, we're also not chickens. Guys, I really just
wanted to get to the other side, the chicken added, but we told the
chicken to hush, we were suspicious of his motives, has he ever
seen a crime show where a witness is in custody and he can't talk
while the cops talk about him, that's kind of what this was like,
so could he just be quiet. The chicken brought up the fact that
was he wasn't in custody and we weren't cops, but we silenced
him, we told him this was martial law, and that flippant attitude
got him into hot water like this in the first place. Edward said
why are we worried about this anyway, just let the chicken cross
the road. We yelled at Edward, we told him it's our right to

inquiry, and why is it his business to make the chicken's decisions for him, what if the chicken doesn't want to cross any more roads. Edward defended himself, saying he never said the chicken wants to or doesn't want to cross other roads, he was just noting it's the chicken's private reasons for crossing the road. Gary stated the road is public property, not private property of the chicken's, so we had a right to question. Edward said nothing's really private property, then Gary told Edward to shut up. Thomas brought up the possibility of the chicken crossing back to the other first side, or even finding another road to cross, we were frightened by the possibility. We decided we were probably going to destroy every road in existence to prevent the chicken from crossing any more roads. The chicken compromised by asking what if he just rode a bike across the road. We thought about this but decided that was still technically crossing the road. The chicken then brought up the possibility of him riding a bus to get where he was going, and we were okay with this. But wait, we stopped, we asked him didn't he originally cross the road just to get to the other side, with no destination in mind? Yes, the chicken became slightly nervous now, but in case of any intentions of him going somewhere, he'd take a bus instead of crossing the road, this comforted us. We said okay, but he better watch what he says about this road incident, next time the state troopers might hear him, and then he'd be in big trouble. Edward said this was ridiculous, to even threaten a chicken like this, we got in Edward's face now, we were talking to the chicken, not him, so could he kindly just butt out. What if it were raining, and the road was slick, and the chicken went to cross the road again, and he slipped and busted his head open, could Edward live with that on his conscience? Edward screamed that if it was raining he doubts the chicken would cross the road or be outside in the first place, and besides there's only a small chance he'd fall. Thomas said why can't the chicken speak for himself, Edward said fine, let the chicken talk, then stepped aside, the chicken said no, he most likely would not cross the road if it was raining, we were dismayed at the "most likely" tag, so the chicken corrected himself and said no, he most definitely would not cross the road in the rain, and we applauded him, that was much better. Edward became disgusted with all of this and crossed the road to leave, we were horrified he'd do such a thing so we all got in our truck and ran him over, and when the chicken went over to check on Edward, we ran him over too, then we collected what was left of him and the eggs he had and made a giant omelet out of it, we're not sure if Edward was in it, it tasted pretty good.

Effect

I was in a room with Winston; a plain room with spooky, unfeeling white walls, a circle of desks and chairs in the middle, with dictionaries and cubbyholes and erasers near the blackboard, on which the phrases "change is important" and "pulp fiction" were written. Winston picked up a marker and wrote "for there to be a plot, characters affect one another". I shot him in the face with my gun.

He was bleeding, there being a spot in his cheek where a hole surrounded by melting-looking skin existed. He somewhat smiled, the crude grin probably because half of his head barely existed now. He reached over and grabbed a knife. He stabbed me in the side. It hurt. Blood poured from my side. I could feel the red fluid flow over my ribs as I hemorrhaged. I shot Winston again.

"Pastries must be microwaved by dogs in blue tutus," I said to him, frowning. Winston just looked at me. Obviously he did not understand the blue tutus were a metaphor for hidden femininity within the construct of his masculine identity; Winston's failure to acknowledge this angered me immensely. I shot him in the kneecap. Winston drooped to one knee. His blood stained the pale grey carpet. A pool of this formed in front of him. Winston stares at it.

This change in verb tense seemed to throw Winston off. He stabs me in the foot with his knife. He doesn't even bother to take it out; instead he just left it in there. I try to fall back in pain but the weapon imbedded in my foot keeps me from stumbling. I remember that I am telling this story in the past tense. My toes snapped from the odd position I was in. The lack of backstory so far disturbs me. I slap Winston; he laughs. Winston has the marker once again and writes "rising action" on the board.

I rip the knife out from my foot. Winston grabs the shotgun. I cleverly note the ironic switch of circumstances. Winston shoots me in the foot now. My foot is damaged beyond repair. This will affect me for the rest of my life; it is a tragedy, like the Greek plays of old, old like my car, which I need to take to the carwash, which reminds me that I need to attend my night college Greek courses. I stab Winston in the forehead.

While blood drips down to the brim of his nose, and drops stain his eyes, Winston says, "To cook, preheat oven to 350 degrees Fahrenheit and stick meal in for forty minutes."

"The current style has moved away from loose-fitting clothes towards more tighter apparel. Oversized cargo pants are out, skinny jeans are in," I exchanged. Winston went to write something on the board. During this distraction I snatch the shotgun from him. For some reason I assume he was going to write "suspense" on the board.

I shoot Winston in the arm. Chunks of his flesh splatter on the wall. "Poppy seeds and chords are laced with vanilla soda on the eve of September," I claim. Winston picks up the knife with one arm, since the art I shot him in is limp and dangling at his side. He slashes me across the face. The cut burns. It doesn't "burn" like fire on my face would. If fire were on my face, say perhaps from mishandling matches, or holding fireworks the wrong way, which happened to a cousin, we called him crazy Timmy, on the fourth of July, I wouldn't be standing here considering it.

Winston lunges forward to stab me in the stomach. "Green cream potato chips Halloween is only celebrated by morose dolphins," he offers as a soul-searching monologue. I sidestep him and shoot him in the ear. We're in the present now. The blast of the shotgun is heard by me, and most likely only me, because Winston's ear is reduced to mangled cartilage now. He kneels on the floor once again, seeming to both laugh and cry. He grabs a copy of T.S. Eliot's collected poems from the shelf and throws it at me. It hits me in the head and knocks me down. Winston writes "meaningful dialogue" on the board.

As I stared at the ceiling I meditate on the popularity of plaid. It is one line of color meets another line of color. What is the sense of this, the allure of such a look? This profound epiphany must be given a voice. I sit up and look at Winston with eager eyes. He slumps against a wall, recovering from his gory wounds. His expression belies one of weariness and dejection; his glazed-over eyes barely seem to meet mine.

"Do you suppose microwaveable pizzas could exist if we didn't have microwaves?" I ask him. "I mean, there would be no practical purpose for them, but they might be a cute commodity. Besides, some people could prefer them frozen." I shoot Winston in the jaw.

He rises to his feet and stabs me in the calf. "Blah blah blah blah blah," he says to me. He slices me in my left breast.

"Blah blah blah blah blah blah blah blah blah," I enunciated to him. I shot him three times, twice in the right cheek and once in the hand.

As he beats me with the blunt end of the knife, he explains to me, "Blah blah blah blah blah blah blah blah blah blah blah blah blah blah blah blah blah blah blah blah blah blah blah blah blah blah blah blah blah blah blah blah blah blah blah blah blah blah blah blah blah blah blah blah blah blah blah blah blah blah blah blah blah blah blah blah blah blah."

I push him off, offended at his criticism of Poe's *Masque of the Red Death*. I shoot him several more times in the back. He lies on the ground seemingly half-paralyzed now; perhaps I penetrated his spine. With a spasm of his arm, for he shakes in a cold sweat, he writes "elements of a scene: time, place, char..." That is as far as he gets. Pointing to the words, he expands on his teachings. "Dwxzy tvche abfwy jnfd owna laewnmc."

"Rozzle mcgoggle wuy vichop tee-lee domy dchtab," I argue with him. The gall of him to argue that Donald Barthelme was a surrealist when he was, in fact, a postmodernist! I shoot him right square in the face. He bleeds like a stuck fish; he falls on the ground and flops around like a pig out of water. I shoot him again. His physiognomy is no longer visible; he is only drenched in a crimson mask. I shoot him several more times. His shirt is demonstrating the seeping through of several mortal wounds.

I shoot Winston once more.

This Story Is So Hipster

Myself, Tom, Stan, and Theodore stood on the edge of the universe, watching the swirling galaxies, the stars, the suns, all of space. Stan sat crouched on an asteroid, his hands to his chin. "Earth, what do you think that is?" he asked.

We all looked around for a minute and it became quite obvious. "Well, Stan, everyone knows it's a planet," I guffawed. "No, no, no," he shook his head, "I know that. But what genre would you classify it under?"

"Genre?" Theodore questioned.

"Yeah, you know. genre. Psychobilly, free jazz, post-rock..." Stan continued.

We all looked at each other in confusion. "Um, I don't know," Tom interjected, "I never really thought about it like that."

We were drifting through space. "I've thought about it for some time," Stan mused, "and in my opinion the whole planet of Earth can correctly be identified as a theatre of the absurd play, because they seem painfully paralyzed and unable to communicate."

"Now, hold on a minute there," I argued, "I have to say ultimately they're a realist work of art, since all that's presented are naturalistic details."

"Oh yeah?" Stan shot back. "Then, how do you explain things like UFOs and Bigfoot?" I stammered a minute. Stan folded his arms across his chest in a smug manner.

"Okay, granted, maybe it has a few magic realist touches, but it's still ultimately realism."

We floated into Earth's atmosphere and arrived near Stonehenge. We observed it for a minute, like a painting in an art gallery. "I feel Stonehenge is postmodern in design and intent. Note the allegorical yet mysterious symbolism, as well as the industrial angles and curves." That was Tom's input. We considered it for a while.

"I have to disagree," Stan announced, head crooked slightly downward with his finger pointing upward, pacing back and forth, as if he were a detective arriving upon some significant clue. "To me, Stonehenge is ultimately a psychological thriller. It presents enough information to let the spectator put the pieces together, ala *The Minus Man* or *Jacob's Ladder*. My feeling is the theme of Stonehenge is truly a summation of existential anguish in the face of contemporary society."

The group looked at each other and nodded their heads. All that was, except me. "Stonehenge, as I see it, is a work wholly embracing the principles of Dada. It has no meaning and comments on the useless absurdity of art and the bourgeois society's attempt to co-opt it."

We all exchanged nods of agreement. With that we made our way over to the country of America, as many works do, debating whether William Shakespeare could ultimately be considered a low-brow or high-brow writer. Stan and myself asserted that Shakespeare employed sexual innuendo and bawdy puns in his plays, which were meant to attract the common audiences and thus underscored the attempt at deeper thematic content, while Tom and Theodore argued that underneath the simple
plotlines, plays such as *Hamlet* and *A Midsummer Night's Dream* addressed universal philosophical issues such as the questioning of one's identity and the balance between order and chaos.

The four of us stopped at an intersection of New York. We turned and looked at a vast crowd who had gathered in a modest square, yelling and waving signs. We thought it was *The Today Show* that fascinated them. "Now this, this crowd, what do you think of them?" I asked everyone.

Theodore was the quickest to respond. "Consulting the critical literature in my research, the crowd gathered here exhibits the traits of transgressive art. You see, through their primal telling and screaming they are attempting to escape the confining norms of their society."

"No, no, no," Tom countered, "if it was transgressive it would be against society. These people are conforming to society by praising popular entertainment. Thus, it is demonstrative of dystopian fiction. Their allegiance to recognizable cultural icons is an ironic commentary on the oppression of humanity, similar to Orwell's *1984*. You could say it has Marxist undertones as well, if you wanted to interpret it that way."

"I see what Tom is saying," Stan added, "but throw in a few zombies and I could easily envisioning this scenario falling under the survival horror genre, which has thrived in cinema but is also associated with video games. You have a mass of people in an urban setting. Obviously it would be a challenge to navigate the city, which is a staple of the style. I imagine the citizens here, if they had to defend themselves against the undead, could acquire a few makeshift weapons."

We grew bored with the crowd of excited onlookers so we continued walking through the busy hustle of the streets of the Big Apple, discussing ways to edit the entries of the place on Wikipedia and TV Tropes when we found the time. Along the way we had a discussion about the ways in which the trash cans of Samuel Beckett's *Endgame* served as metaphors. Stan and Theodore claimed they represented oblivion and the mortal fate awaiting all of us, while Tom and myself deduced it really had no further context and that they were what they were. As we finished our analysis we came upon a few construction workers reconfiguring the pavement on a road. The one who drew our attention wore an orange vest and a yellow hardhat. His white and brown plaid shirt was tucked into a pair of muddied blue jeans. His grey mustache sharply contrasted with his black boots. The sound of his jackhammer against the concrete produced a shrill, sonic dissonance.

"If I had to give a label to this sound, it would be grindcore," Tom began. "It has a heavy, harsh sound, with brief blasts of noise. If you truly listen though, underneath there is a melody to it, though it's incredibly fast-paced. The lack of other sounds places the main focus on the jackhammer's thrashing auditory assault."

"Wrong, Tom," Theodore cut in. "This sounds exactly like death metal to me. Grindcore is more about the tempo, whereas death metal is about the overall sound. And as you can hear, the quality of the jackhammer's sound is quite abrasive."

The man stared at us for a second as he kept at his job. A beeping could be heard; we turned our heads and saw a bulldozer slowly backing up. "The addition of another instrument, courtesy of this electronic device, signifies this as an industrial piece. It is not music as one usually thinks of it, but rather comprised of mechanical beats using different, non-standard instruments," I surmised. The men at the helms of both the jackhammer and the bulldozer stopped for a minute to converse with each other. The man operating the bulldozer then walked away. The man with the jackhammer drank a bit of coffee. After he finished, he continued his work, albeit on a different part of the ground, which produced a slightly different sound.

"Aha!" Stan exclaimed. "All three of you are incorrect. The different sound here signifies this is progressive. It is actually a few songs in one. Note the slight variation in pitch and time signature, as well as the inclusion of multiple instruments. The long pace and odd, ethereal sounds harken back to prog rock, in a similar vein to Pink Floyd's *Dark Side of the Moon*."

We watched him continue for a few minutes, then moved on. As the four of us continued we passed through various states like Virginia, Oklahoma, and Ohio. Deciding to venture outside of the United States, we flew through the air a bit, scanning for countries to land in. Settling on Japan, we gently descended upon the ground, coming to a schoolyard. The students were heading back to their classrooms, likely having been on a lunch break. On one of the tables in the courtyard we found an open notebook one of them left behind. It had several sketches in it.

Holding it up above his head for all of us to see, Stan kicked off the debate. "This is a striking example of impressionism to me. Note the smudged artwork and the lack of truly realistic details. The picture here, which appears to be a dragon and a small schoolgirl, is recorded as if one viewed it in an instant. There are traces now of bright artwork, which no doubt will soon be completed."

I stepped in next. "Stan, your label of 'impressionism' shows that you fall into the usual trap of seeing everything through the lens of Western culture. Keep in mind the location we are in and its inherent influences." I took the notebook from his hands and stared at it. "This is clearly hentai to me. It mixes the supernatural with the ordinary in an enigmatic, suggestive way. The expression on the girl's face, as well as the presence of the dragon, carries strong sexual undertones to me. Note the detail afforded to the dragon's features, including his scales and tail, as well as the exaggerated expression on the girl's face."

"My perspective is a bit different from both of you," Theodore said. "I think you're reading too much into the supposed sexual currents. I would say this is a shining example of deconstruction. The dragon and the young schoolgirl are not supposed to be seen in an erotic light but more so in terms of gender identities. Though dragons are usually associated with aggressive masculinity and schoolgirls with timid femininity, by placing them together, the illustrator is attempting to break the gender divide, as Derrida predicted. This sketch also juxtaposes two unlike objects in an attempt to shake people out of the usual constructed narratives they inhabit."

Tom took some time to think all of this over and then concluded we each had equally valid points. We traveled around a bit, exploring the bottom of the ocean and finding different animals down there, trying to figure out what species they belonged to. We came back up to the surface after a few hours and finally came to a topic we could truly have a heated debate about. "George Washington--now, what subculture did he belong to?" Theodore began. "In my opinion he was undeniably a hippie. He had a disregard for fashion which is augmented by his shabby style of dress. His hair was long and he carried on an anti-establishment credo which included disdain for overbearing authority and the church. As well, his ultimate goal was the achievement of utopian ideals, an optimism which hippies embrace wholeheartedly."

"If I had to classify Washington, I would place him under the grunge moniker," Tom deduced. "His careless appearance stemmed from his bleak depression. He was known to have a hatred of crowds and to be wary of politics, themes which often arise in alternative rock lyrics. Since they didn't have adequate showers back then, I'm sure his hygiene was less than adequate. And while heroin wasn't invented back then, rumors have swirled George was an opium addict, and possibly enjoyed marijuana."

"Both of you are incorrect," Stan claimed. "George Washington was ultimately a punk. The so-called long hair was just a wig; in reality, he had short hair, which punks prefer. Another punk quality about him is he preferred active revolution. He saw violence and conflict as the solution to social problems, which the punk culture also tends to advocate. His appearance was messy, but more of a extravagant and theatrical type, which is a third feature of punk rock."

"Actually, I'd say he was a hipster," I joined in. "Punks tend to be more anarchist and Washington obviously set up the framework for our current government, so we can disqualify that moniker right away. He was in fact the first to advocate for democracy, and if he were around today, he'd surely tout how he was into it before everyone else. Also, as far as his fashion sense, he mixed so-called 'sloppy' rebellion with aristocratic and high-end aesthetics, a balance which hipsters aim for. He also enjoyed irony, since he owned slaves despite being against the idea. Some biographies allege he was into obscure classic music that no one else of his time knew about and that he enjoyed a certain specific strain of ale similar to how hipsters have branded PBR as their go-to drink."

We all nodded our heads in agreement. Soon we grew tired with the ground and wandered up into the atmosphere. After hopping back and forth between clouds we settled on one we

really liked and sat on it as it drifted. "So what does everyone think of this story?" I began. "I would say, at its heart, this piece of literature is an absurdist work of satire. Our exaggerated analysis of everything we encounter, which ridicules the current propensity to label and classify all works of art, is heightened by hyperbolic dialogue and diction. As well, our improbable actions, such as existing in outer space and the
fact that we're sitting on this cloud, lends to it an extreme disregard for the tenets of standard slice-of-life fiction."

Stan smacked his lips. He was always the dissenter. "While it certainly has absurdist elements to it, this short story could be called surrealist as well. The dreamlike elements of the narrative, such as our casual discussions about eccentric matters and the physically impossible settings and actions that you mention earlier, give this an odd, otherworldly feeling. The events brought up are random and seemingly disjointed, and do not point to a unifying theme or overarching idea."

Tom jumped in. "This story involving us isn't surrealist because if truly were in the vein of Salvador Dali or Andre Breton, I wouldn't be speaking in this sentence right now, with coherent syntax. It would be completely chaotic and unconscious and wouldn't be a true story, per se. The author here seems to be writing from a romanticist perspective. True, he is less concerned with realism and the usual constraints of fiction, but only as a means of expressing pure emotion. We are not well-developed characters but rather simplified archetypes through which he expresses his views, which is in line with the romanticist style. As well, there is a theme of upheaval against societal standards, especially in regards to championing the common feeling man as opposed to our collegiate snobbery. William Blake and Walt Whitman are influences in this regard."

As we passed over the Atlantic Ocean I suggested we leave Earth and go back into space. As we toured about the galaxy we found a new model to classify: the universe itself. "The cosmos are, once and for all, belonging to the mod counterculture," Theodore chimed in. All of creation is intensely structured and stylized, mirroring the mod preoccupation with manner and dress. "At times, this meticulousness seems to carry a tone of droll whimsy, considering the amount of tragedy, suffering, and emptiness contained here in the galaxies."

Tom offered up his theory. "I would say the universe is emo. While it is concerned primarily with appearance, this underscores a sense of dramatic pain and suffering. Everything is inherently internalized and melodramatic with this sense of struggle. Notice the majority of people cry or become despondent when confronted with evil and disappointment. The whole universe is organized around a tight time-space continuum...much like emo apparel is tight."

Stan stepped in the middle and made his announcement. "The universe is not so much emo but more gothic. Many people tend to confuse these terms and think they are interrelated but they are completely separate movements. Look around you...space is completely black. As you know, the gothic culture tends towards all-black clothing and apparel of darker color, though this is neither exclusive to the scene nor a sweeping definition of what is goth. Far from weakness in the face of adversity, I think the universe and the inhabitants within it cultivate not only a strength by bathing in darkness, but also there is an enigmatic mystique surrounding these matters, an aura which the goth culture tends to project. The universe stretches back millions and millions of years, mimicking the goth fascination with the ancient, arcane, and quaint."

We all nodded our heads in agreement.

The Form Must Be Signed At Eleven

The form must be signed at eleven, or so the woman behind the counter has told me. I get there around ten or so to give me time to talk to her again. When I reached her on the phone she told me it might be a ten minute wait in line. So I rush over there and park my car in the lot and hurry over to the building where she told me I'd have to go. Throwing open the door, I see there's about six or seven people in line. There's a velvet rope to guide everyone along while they stand there with their arms folded. Inside the building is gray, with the assistants hidden behind glass windows. There's a vent in which they call out for the next person in line. Walking up, I stand behind a tall guy. Checking my watch, I see now that it's 10:03.

After slowly inching up for what seems like forever I get to the window. Hiding behind it is a stout woman seated at a desk. I glance behind her and her office seems to be filled with cabinets. On her desk are a few papers. "May I help you?" she barks in a flat tone.

"Yes, I'm here to return this form." I take it out my back pocket, unfold it, and slide it under the window. She seems to wince at it being slightly crumpled. "We talked on the phone this morning," I offer. She says nothing of that.

Going over it with her finger, she smacks her lips as she reads the signatures on it. "This is the wrong form," she declares.

"What? But I thought that was the one I needed!" I exclaim.

"No. You need form A. This is form C." She places it behind her. "If you go down to the corrections office, they still have them on hold."

"Where's that at?"

"If you go out this door, down the hall, then hang a left, take a right, climb up the stairs, take the elevator, and go all the way to the end, it's the door on the right." She takes a sip of her water. "It's not
too hard to find." Waving me away, she calls out, "Next!"

So I go out the door, hang a left, take a right, climb up the stairs, take the elevator, and look for the door on the right, all the way at the end. The only thing is, the hallway seems endless. There are rows and rows of doors, all of which look just like each other. The fluorescent light seems to cast a dim glow on the floors, which look quite shiny. When I check my watch it says it's 10:06. Not too bad. I'm making some time, I think to myself.

Walking down the hallway, I scan through the doors, trying to guess which one she meant. They are all slightly ajar. When I try to peek in I catch a glimpse of a chair. I start to huff when I finally make it to the end of the hallway. There's one last door on the right. Hopefully this is it. It has no cover, just a dark brown wooden door with a slightly rusty knob. Raising my hand up, I hesitate to knock on it. What if it's the wrong door and I bother this person? But I force myself to meekly knock on it. No answer. I wait a minute and knock on it again. This time a hand reaches through and gently opens it.

"Yes?" a man sitting at a desk says. His hair is short and thin, he has a neatly-trimmed beard, and he wears a navy blue suit. He sits hunched in his seat, seeming to pour over a few papers.

"Hi. Is this the corrections office?" I ask.

"Yes." He peers up at me. "Can I be of assistance?" he utters.

"I need form A."

"You don't already have form A?"

"No, I had form C. The lady from the main office sent me over here," I protest, waving around the form.

"Okay. Settle down," he huffs. He turns around in his chair, opens a few drawers, and fumbles around. "Here it is. Form A. Only a few of these left." He takes out a form that looks similar to the one I already have, except the letterhead is in the upper left-hand corner. He hands it to me. "You do know you have to get this signed by the sub-officer, right?"

"What?" I shriek. "Sub-officer?"

He grumbles. "Do you know anything?" He rubs his forehead. "If you go across the field her office is about five minutes away from here." He looks at the clock on his desk. "Isn't the deadline at eleven?"

"Yeah," I affirm, with one foot already in the hallway.

"Well, I'd get moving if I was you." With that, he lowers his eyes back to his previous task.

Now I make a dash for the field, which is an open expanse of green grass. As I hurry I peek a quick glance at my watch; it's now 10:10. If I hurry I can make all this in time, I think to myself. Yeah, despite all these setbacks, I'm still making good on schedule. Plenty of time to talk to this person and get all this sorted out. No problem. I scuffle along the field, which is somewhat hilly and has a few odd bumps here and there. I make sure to avoid an anthill and spot a large brown building which is a bit far off. I pass up a parking lot, which is full of cars that gleam in the afternoon sunlight.

There are four rows of steps to climb up. I make it up the first one and nearly slip since I am walking so fast. It's hot and my clothes start to cling to me since I begin sweating. When I look at the ground there are a few cracks in the ground. Weeds are starting to grow there. Making it up the second and third steps, I pause to catch my breath. There are about thirty steps for each row. I finally get to the top and observe the building before me rather quickly. The gray sign at the top is mounted on a few thin black wires and says simply in large white letters "Office of Sub-Divisions". The building itself is composed of bland brown bricks and stands far above the rest of the structures in this area. I look at myself in the glass of the door; my hair is now a bit frazzled and my face is red. But I don't care. I'm not here to look good, I just need to get this form signed. The windows are sleek but don't let you see what is inside. They only dimly reflect the outside world.

Going to open the door, it won't budge. It must be locked. Looking closer, I see that there is a keypad to the right of

the handle. "Damn it," I grumble to myself. That guy didn't say I needed a code
to get in. I just need to get this fucking form signed and...

"What are you here for?" a voice booms out. There's a bit of feedback towards the end. Glancing up, I don't see anyone around. It must be through a loudspeaker.

"Um, hi," I make a stab at formality. "Are you the sub-officer?"

"Yes." Her voice is shrill but commanding.

"The corrections office sent me over here. I need you to sign form A." I grasp it in my hand, seeing that the edges are now slightly drenched with perspiration.

There is a brief pause. "Come in."

Once again reaching out, I find the door pulls open this time. When I step inside, I see the building is not only very large but also mostly empty. The hallway stretches out for about a mile or so. In the far right corner is the beginning of a stairway. In the middle are a set of doors. Next to that is a vending machine. I have no idea where to go or where the sub-officer is. Strolling about, I check my watch. 10:24. Scanning the walls, I see a sign on the wall that looks like a map. Moving closer, I see it's a black plaque with a star labeled "You are here" in the middle. Surrounding that are little squiggles that all loop into each other. I trace my finger and look for where the sub-officer is located. Apparently it's on the third floor. Heading towards the stairway, I start to climb that. The steps snake from left to right. When I hit the second floor I come simply to a wall. "What the hell?" I yell, and lightly pound the wall with my fist. A jolt of pain rises up in my arm and I rush back down to where I started. This time I see a path at the other end of the hallway that seems to lead to another part of the building. I amble on through that and find yet another seemingly endless set of doors, none of which are labeled. I knock on one of them randomly, hoping for someone to come out and tell me something. No answer.

I make it to the other side of the building and find yet another stairway. Even though I have a feeling this one will lead nowhere, I decide to give it a try. Clutching the railing, I find this one does have a second floor. I walk in and see a receptionist sitting at a desk. There a few chairs set against the wall and a stack of magazines on a table. The carpet is a dark shade of maroon. The temperature feels a bit chilly since they probably have the air conditioning on constantly. Behind her people sit in chairs and stare at blank computer monitors. She makes a few clicks and chews some gum, not noticing me.

I subtly walk up to her. "Hi."

She seems startled by my presence. "How did you get in here?"

"The sub-officer let me in here." I gulp. "I think."

"Have you made an appointment?"

Grimacing, I reply, "No." I hold up form A. "But the corrections office sent me over here. They told me I need to have the sub-officer sign this before I turn it in."

She smacks her lips. Her hair is red and done up in curls. She wears a white cardigan and has small gold earrings. On her desk is presumably a picture of her and some family members on a fishing trip. "They didn't call us and tell us." She picks up the phone and presses a button. "One minute, please." She listens for a second, then whispers, "There's someone here to see you. About form A?" She clutches the phone to her ear with both hands. "Okay." She hangs it up and looks at me. "The sub-officer can see you, but she has other obligations at the minute. It'll be a twenty minute wait."

I take a seat and flip through some magazines which are several hundred years out of date. They're pamphlets from the eighteenth century, in fact. I check my watch. It's now 10:35. Fuck, the deadline is coming up soon and I really just have to get this thing turned in. Finally, after what seems like an eternity, the receptionist simply gives me the thumbs up. As I make a mad dash for the sub-officer's office she calls out behind me, "Do you know where it is?" I don't respond to her.

I finally find where the sub-officer's office is. The only way to really get to it is to take an elevator. I walk over to it. The doors are somewhat uneven to each other, a few sparks of electricity light up at the top, and the panel appears rusted, with the buttons of it worn. I go to touch it with my fingers and feel it fall a little. An uneasy feeling settles in my stomach. Rubbing my forehead, I desperately look around. The office is just one floor above this. There's a window with a bit of a ledge that maybe I can scale. No, no, that's crazy talk. But this elevator appears broken. Walking towards it, I see the ledge actually appears to have enough room for me to climb on. Peering upwards, I see there's a ladder that leads to the third floor. It's a crazy idea but what other way do I have in? The ladder leads up to a window on the third floor.

The window opens when I give it a try, which is a good sign. I gingerly step out onto the ledge and feel my heart flutter. Leaving the window open since I can't reach around and close it, I desperately grasp a pipe near me to maintain my balance. A slight breeze kicks in, which makes me nervous. I take a few steps towards the left and find I can walk fine if I'm slow about it. After a quick walk I get to the ladder. Reaching out with my left hand, I shift my body weight and make it to the ladder. Even though I should know not to I quickly peer down; I'm a good distance from the ground. Looking back up, I see it's only a few rungs to the third floor window, which hopefully opens. Each climb I make I get closer to the third floor. Finally making it up, I reach for the latch and find, to my luck, the window opens. Yes!

I climb inside, looking around to make sure no one catches me. Once again, the floor is completely empty and almost eerily quiet. It looks a bit like the second floor, except in the corner are a few plush red chairs. The floor on this level is a shiny marble. Perhaps it has been recently waxed. But I don't have time to wonder about stuff like that. Checking my watch, I see it's 10:45. Crap. If I hustle I can get back in time. I walk forward until I see a stand that says in bright green letters "The Sub-Officer's Office" with an arrow pointing forward. I run over in that direction. At the end of the hallway is a room with the doors open. The walls and the floors appear completely white. The sub-officer stands there, a slightly elderly woman with light blond hair, wrinkles dotting her face, thick eye shadow, and a beige blazer to complement her brown skirt. I forego knocking since she is already starting me down by the time I make it to her office.

"Do you have form A?" she simply says.

"Yes," I huff, holding it up in front of her.

"You do know about the dragon, right?" she states flatly.

"Dragon?"

"Anyone who wishes to have a form signed by the sub-officer must defeat a dragon in combat." She matches my look of utter disbelief with, "We recently made this change to our guidelines two years ago. It seems to be mostly successful." She walks behind her desk and produces a silver sword from her wall. "Good luck."

Handing me the weapon, she steps aside and as I look to the left of her room I find it actually stretches out into a dusky medieval-era dungeon. There's the slight sound of water dripping, dirty stone to substitute for a floor, and gothic architecture that just out the walls. From the shadows emerges a rather large green dragon. His skin is scaly, his ears droop but are pointy, his eyes are bright orange, and a few miniscule flames escape his mouth as he breathes, letting out a shrill shriek as he views me. I gulp and utter "Jesus Christ" before glancing back at the sub-officer, who only shrugs and smiles.

Raising the sword up, I figure I have nothing else to do but charge. The dragon stoops down and swats me away with his tail, which sends me flying into the wall. My back is now racked with pain but I stumble up and this time hop onto his tail as he makes another strike, quickly grabbing onto his skin as I gradually ascend his body until I reach his face and stab his eyes out. The dragon screams in agony as I hack away at him, blood pouring everywhere. As he starts to fall down I slash away at his throat for good measure. He seems mostly dead and I brace myself as he finally falls to the ground, a heavy cloud of dust kicking up at his corpse. Throwing the sword aside, I stare a hole through the sub-officer as she picks up form A from her desk and signs it. "You have a great day," she says as I leave her office. I wouldn't mind taking that sword to her but perish the thought as I snatch it back and start back to the main office to turn this stupid thing in.

It's all the way on the other side so I run faster than I ever have in my life, but have to stop to catch my breath. I even vomit once since I'm so dehydrated by this point. On the way over there I check my watch again, trying not to get too distracted to where I run into anything. 10:56. Almost there. If I can just make it...

I finally spot it. The same nondescript building as ever. The inside doesn't look crowded at all, probably because it's about to close. But this time a few security guards seem to dot the outside. There's two on each end, both of them wearing navy blue track jackets, blue hats with the word "Security" on them in yellow lettering, sunglasses, and black khaki pants. One of them has a beard. They stand still with their arms folded behind their back but say something into their walkie-talkies when they spot me coming near. "Excuse me, but you do know the building is about to close, right?" one of them says, his voice harsh and raspy.

"Yeah, I know. I just need to turn this form in," I pant, waving the form in front of their face.

"Oh, form A. You do know you need to pay the fee before you turn it in, right?"

"Fee?" My teeth clench together now.

"Yes. It's a fifty dollar charge to pay. It's listened under the information section on the website." He eyes me up and down. "You should have read."

I left everything besides my ID and keys in my car so I curse and rush back to my car, desperately searching in the glove box for my wallet and hope I have enough in there to pay this crummy charge. I whisk out two twenties and a ten (luckily I went to the bank yesterday to withdraw some money) and hurry back. When I go to hand the security guard the money he already has his hand out. He skims through the money and nods. "I'm sorry, sir. The building has just closed. And the deadline has also passed." I check my watch. It's now eleven o'clock.

Science Fiction

I want to tell a story. But I'm not sure what kind of story. Perhaps a science fiction story. I could have aliens and explosions and hostile intergalactic takeovers. No, no, that's been done before. It's treaded ground. But aren't all stories subjects that have been covered before? A lot of stories done before have had a male narrator or protagonist. So perhaps I'll have a hermaphroditic narrator or protagonist.

So I won't do a science fiction story. I'll do a realistic story. I can include dogs and grass and garbage and pavement. But perhaps that would be too boring. People could find these things in everyday life. They read fiction to escape. Novels are a window into another world. Why would they want to read a realistic story then? But perhaps all fiction stems from what the writer knows. And I know reality. Besides, by virtue of being creations of mine, these "realistic" characters are windows into another world. Even science fiction can be boiled down to a basic human element. Man, why do I keep coming back to science fiction? I should make obsession a part of my story. Zelda tells me I write too much about obsession.

Why do I want to tell a story? Never mind the surface reason like the themes I want to develop, like say "good and evil are necessary", I've done a few stories like that, but not to digress, because I know that will lose a reader. Zelda says it loses her sometimes. But why, at this precise moment in time, do I want to tell a story? Why does anyone want to tell a story? Too many questions. This is supposed to be a story. Simple, short, declarative statements. Zelda says I ask too many questions.

By now you, whoever you are that's reading this, may be wondering who Zelda is. Such a mysterious character. I keep mentioning her and I don't explain who she is. Maybe she's not even a character at all. Perhaps she's fake, a figment of my imagination. After all, so far she's just a name. But no, she is a character--for the purposes of this story, which is not the story I want to tell. I'm not even sure if this a story at all. I'm sorry, I keep rambling on...I'm a terrible narrator. Zelda is an identity. Zelda is a person. She is a fully rounded and three dimensional character with desires, motivations, and complex thoughts. Zelda is my wife.

You know what, I never answered the question of why I want to write a story. It's not fair to dangle an important part of the plot in front of the reader like that and then drop it. That's sloppy writing. Although some fiction enjoys leaving the questions it brings up unanswered as a metaphor for the existential ambiguities of life and yada yada yada. Zelda is annoyed by literature like that. I never got around to elaborating on Zelda, have I? Right now she is tending to the baby, the one we had a year ago. Today she's worn a dark green cardigan sweater and brown khaki pants. She gave the baby, whose name is Doyle, a bottle of milk and then sang him a lullaby.

How shall I write this story? Should it be in first person? Or third person? What about present tense? Or past tense? What is most science fiction narrated in? I'm trying to remember if *War of the Worlds* was present tense or past tense. Is there a future tense? "He will go to the river bank"? Christ, there's all these questions. Who am I asking them to? Myself? Obviously. No else will read this story. Yet earlier I made reference to "you". Maybe it's a hypothetical second person I conjured up, as an internal mental voice to myself. You know how you talk to yourself? I mean not talk to yourself in a crazy way (or schizophrenia if you want to be nice) but how you always have that reading voice that goes off in your head that's on all the time? You can tell mine is active. Anyway...I lost my train of thought. Oh yeah, is this a story? A story needs time, place, characters, events, and action. Things happening. A story cannot take place entirely with someone's thoughts. This isn't even my story. It's my memoir. Maybe.

I don't see how I can figure out how to write a story if I'm not even sure what to write. I need to forget about science fiction. It's a hackneyed genre. There are no deep themes to be found from it. I need to be my own writer. I can't copy from other people. That's a recipe for downfall. I do like writing things dramatically like that though: "recipe for downfall". It sounds cool. Is that the direction I should go in? That could be my voice. Even if other writers have been dramatic like that before.

Eh, I'm not so sure now. Zelda says that's one of my flaws. I told her she can be a bit harsh. So then we got into a fight, which happens sometimes. Anyway, back to the science fiction. I'm drawn to that and I don't know why. I can explore that as a motif with my story as a way to work it out. Then when it's published I can deny it to all my family and friends and readers. If I get readers. How do you get them? So what do I want in my science fiction story...how about other planets? I can reasonably picture what they look and act like. I can also have UFOs. There's plenty of information online I can search about in regards to them. But how do I know aliens exist? What they look like? Is it because of what other people have told me? Do I even believe aliens exist (it's something I honestly haven't given much thought to before)? Perhaps knowledge is the sum of the individual. But nonetheless people might be able to relate to my story. Even if they've never seen aliens or even abducted by one, they can imagine it. Isn't that what all fiction is really, imagination?

Plus aliens are such an established pop culture mainstay people already bring their opinions into it. Also, science fiction is a very well-selling genre. People love that sense of foreign adventure. Same with fantasy, but I'm not as into that. Am I doing this just for money? I do love to write. But I also want some sort of income. I've complained before about being a starving artist despite making money at my day job (as a copywriter, in case you're curious) while being self-aware of what a trite stereotype it is. So I obviously do it for the love and passion of it. At the same time, I do want my stuff to be marketable and reach a wide audience so I have the funds to do it. It seems this a tightrope all writers and artists walk. I say "seems" because I honestly don't know too many other artists

and writers. When I tell Zelda these thing she says to keep at my dreams but also be realistic, especially since we have a kid to support. Most of the time she doesn't relate since she works in the healthcare industry. Which is fine. I'm not totally against that. It's a good, steady job and I guess people need medical care. I just don't
personally understand it.

But enough about Zelda. Back to the main topic. Why am I so hung up on a science fiction? Perhaps it's a metaphor for something. Most literature has metaphors. Maybe it doesn't mean anything at all. That would be very anti-art and experimental. Zelda doesn't understand most of the avant-garde stuff I show her. But no matter what, I do want to have some sort of plot in my story. It is important for fiction to have something happening. I need imagery, dialogue, and character interactions and events to accomplish all this. Don't you just hate short stories where nothing really happens?

This seems to be going nowhere. I shouldn't be worried about it, though. This is not the story I want to tell. With the story I want to tell I will focus on that and have it more organized. Or perhaps it won't be organized at all. It can be a modernist work of art, reflecting the confused and jumbled nature of the world. Rather, it won't be unorganized, but organized in an unorganized manner. I'm confusing myself again. Perhaps I'll just have it organized after all.

Do you think I could mix and match? Maybe I can include an autobiographical account in the science fiction story. *Slaughterhouse Five* had that. Kurt Vonnegut included that in his science fiction piece. I think science fiction fails when it doesn't relate its extraordinary occurrences to a basic human element. That seems to be where all fiction fails.

Look at me, babbling on about abstract things. I sound like some sort of philosopher. I need more concrete things. I need solid, tangible sensory details. I need cars and shoes and cats and one person approaching the other. This person, the approacher, will look at the approachee dead in the eye, his black pupils a minute dot compared to the icy blue rings that give him a chilling demeanor. The other person, the approachee, will give the man with blue irises a quizzical look. He knows this man, he is a shadow from the past, back when he lived in the rural country. The first man, the approacher, smirks and reaches into his pocket for something.

Scratch that. That beginning was egregious (which is a good word). It was overly dramatic. I'm not even sure where to take that that story. This is all so pointless. I'm a horrible writer. I'm one of the worst writers ever. I know every writer says that but I truly believe it. I could never compare to Faulkner or Dostoevsky or Hemingway. Why am I even a writer? It's not really productive. It's kind of a lazy and bizarre job if you think about it (if you could even call it a "job"). I should just switch to being an engineer or a construction worker. I'd never get published. And even if I did, do you think I'd ever make any money or get famous? Look at this. I can't even tell a story, which is perhaps a story about not being able to tell stories. I'm confusing myself. I suck. I should just give this up. Zelda talks me out of it a bit but also reminds me I chose a difficult path in life.

Alright, so aliens invade Earth because a subliminal stream in their water supply convinces them...eh, forget it. This is crap. I'm crap. Why are writers always so depressed and tough on themselves? Zelda's right. After I write these very words I'm going to ball up this story and throw it in the trash. This isn't even a story at all.

The Caveman Waits In Line

"Next in line, please!" Krug the teller said. The red tie around his neck seemed slightly lost amid his thick, brown, curly chest hair, his wild and unkempt beard, and his drooping brow. Oog walked up from the line of smelly patrons clad in singlets (97% silk, 3% cotton). "Hello, me like to cash this check." Oog handed it over to Krug.

Krug took a look at it, being careful not to scrape it with his long fingernails. "Do you have account with this bank?"

Oog looked puzzled. "No, but me would like to start account with bank."

Krug handed the check back to Oog. The bank was tastefully furnished, with concrete desks and benches for patrons of the establishment. The cave it was fashioned out of was lit in strategic places with lamps, with tasteful paintings far off in the corner. "I'm sorry, you must stand over there to start account. Thank you and have a..."

"But me need to cash check. Me need money."

"You must have account to cash check."

"Me cash check!" Oog screamed. He jumped on top of the desk and banged his fists, yelling the whole time. Security came by and escorted him from the building.

Bog walked over to the middle of a barren field as a group of people followed him. He turned and faced them. The area where they stood was an arid, empty space, save for a few shrubs and trees. The dust flew past their feet as a slight wind kicked up. "Thank you, ladies and gentlemen for joining me here today. Let me, first of all, say me appreciate interest and sacrifice so far as it relates to this endeavour. What we are on the verge of is an exciting new prospect."

He took a gulp, then continued. "Fine Inc. plans to expand its empire by building yet another franchise here, in the middle of area. The fact that this area is vastly underpopulated will cut down costs associated with building and maintaining it, thus maximizing revenue. Now, any questions before we continue?" A woman carrying a club (which was decorated with a few diamonds) raised her hand. Bog's eyebrows, which were thick compared to the rest of his head, raised up as he took an interest in her. "Yes, you have question?"

"Yes, just one. Isn't this area notorious for being populated with dinosaurs? The idea of building a store here seems a bit dangerous to me."

A few seconds of silence lapsed as Bog raised his heavy arms to bring his hands to his chin. "Good question. Me would just like to state that the rumors of this area being populated by dinosaurs is false. As you all know, dinosaurs died out a while ago. There is no risk of danger at all. We are completely committed to the safety of our customers and employees." With that, they heard a roar behind them. As Bog and the whole group turned around, they saw a T-Rex charging towards them.

Oog stood in line at the college bookstore. Shelves and shelves of books spanned the place, some of which were *Premodern Theory of the Role of the Woman in Contemporary Rock Carvings and Wall Paintings* and *Put Down the Mastodon Ribs: A Guide to Better Living Through a Paleolithic Diet and You.* The man in front of him huffed and grumbled. "Next," the cashier announced. Hidden among his long, frizzy mane were a pair of glasses. He wore a light green button up shirt, which was tucked into a tight pair of black trousers.

"Yeah, me like to sell these books back," Oog told him, dumping a whole bunch of books on the man's desk.

He analyzed them and went through them one by one. "None of these can be sold back."

"What? Why?"

"Overstock. We can't take them."

"But I paid nearly four hundred lion teeth for them!"

"I'm sorry. But we're swamped right now." He flipped through the last book of Oog's stack. "We can take this one." He punched in a few keys on the stick computer. "This is worth 3 lion's teeth and a leaf." He handed the currency to Oog.

"That's it? That book was so expensive!"

"Thank you and have a good day!"

Oog stormed out of the bookstore and began jumping up and down in the hallway.

Jud walked to the podium, which was in actuality just a rock, and gleamed out into the audience of reporters, ready to chisel his every word on their tablets. "Welcome, everyone. First of all, let me just say I want to thank everyone for being here. I, today, would like to announce I am throwing my hat in the race and will be a candidate for the 108 B.V. tribe leader. As a representative for the Hunter Party, I feel I can reinvigorate our direction and provide a strong opposition to the Gatherer Party. My public relations assistant, Dion, will be here to explain my platform."

Dion walked over, dressed in a leopard skin skirt and high heels which were made out of bamboo. "Hello. It has been an honor working alongside Mr. Jud. I feel he is a charismatic man of the people. which is why I chose to direct his campaign. One area we want to focus on is the issue of meat. Whereas previous candidates supported a more aggressive means of hunting for food, I wanted to emphasize Mr. Jud's more nuanced view of this matter. Since he feels we already have a surplus of food and clothing, we should not hunt any more unless absolutely necessary. To do so would be the big tribe mentality trying to infringe on our individual rights. We also need to cut down on the funds we spend, especially in regards to spears and hammers. Mr. Jud is also a family man, evidenced by the fact that he will not eat children when rations get low..."

"What about health care costs for the elderly?" one reporter interjects. "Statistics show the average life expectancy is now expected to rise to thirty-five years old."

Oog took a seat in the conference room, where moss dangled from the walls in arranged displays and a hastily carved sign reading in huge letters, "At Stone-A-Center, you're #1!" The chair, with its glued-together sticks of wood, was slightly uncomfortable, but Oog beared with it. The manager, a tall, husky man with a nametag that said Grug, and a few gobs of goo in his hair that were arranged in a slight comb-over, strolled in, offering a smile that highlighted his few jagged teeth.

Grug extended his hairy palm to Oog. "Hello, Oog. Pleasure to meet you."

"Same here. Let me say me am thankful for this opportunity."

"Oh, no problem. Now..." Grug took a seat across from him. "Let me just go through some preliminary procedures. These questions are part of the hiring process." Grug flipped through his clipboard, the weathered bits of parchment holding on as he turned the pages. "First question: what do you feel separates you from the competition?" Grug's eyes narrowed as he said the last words of his question.

Oog's eyes shot up at the ceiling as he took a moment to ponder his answer. "Well, me have to say my main asset is my ability to walk upright, which me have acquired in recent years. Me feel this is an advantage I have over other prospective employees. For one, it allows me to reach for items on the higher shelves, whereas those that are still hunched over wouldn't be able to do so."

"Alright. Very good point." Grug made a note on the pad with his stylus. "Question two: describe a previous experience where you and your co-workers worked together to avoid a potential hazard."

Oog nodded his head and pursed his lips in a smug manner. "Well, with my previous job at the bronze mill, one day a tiger had wandered in and began terrorizing everyone. In fact, it ate our boss, which really cut down productivity for that day. Anyway, everyone else panicked, but seeing as me had to regularly fend them off while staying with my family in my cave, me felt prepared to take charge. Me had a few of the other workers distract the tiger while me pushed the tiger into a tar pit. It slowly sank and died. We were then able to get back to business as usual."

Gruh coughed. "Yes. That's something that's the cornerstone of any business, working together to correct a potential safety hazard." He made another note with his stylus. "Well, that's it for the first part of this interview. I'll lead you to the regional manager, who wants to talk to you as well." The two of them stood up. "But personally, I'll highly recommend you. You strike me as a good fit here. Thank you for your time."

"Thank you as well," Oog said as he left to walk out the door. As he navigated his way through the building, Oog growled excitedly and beat his fists against the wall.

Bod bellowed through the small tube in his hand. "Me say, let Ra, the sun god, into your life. All the pain and suffering you feel will be cleansed. Just say, Ra, save me." The cloak he wore was of a bright green color and his hair was combed back. He held his arms to the air in a dramatic pose. The crowd of people by him did the same and murmured to themselves.

"You, ma'am, come up here." He pointed to an elderly woman who walked with a shabby shuffle. "Come on, now, come talk to me." As she warbled up there, he took her gently by the wrist and helped her up to the platform of smooth rocks. "Tell me about the hurt in your life." He stuck the hollowed-out tube near her face.

"Well, our tribe was out hunting one day and the mammoth we tried to bring down stomped on me. I survived but now I can barely walk." There was an inflection of sad longing in her voice.

"I'm very sorry to hear that. But you know what?" Bod paced back and forth theatrically. "Ra has a plan for you. He has a plan for all of us. And through the power of Ra, I will heal you. Hold back your head." As the woman gained a curious look on her face, the preacher placed his hand over her head and began babbling incoherently. "Let Ra in! Let the spirit of Ra in!" She, too, began uttering gibberish.

"This woman is saved! Can you walk now?" She got up and, to her astonishment, could walk. As she pranced off the stage, a grin came over Bod's face. "See what happens when you let the sunlight in? The sun is out every day, it keeps us warm, it allows us to see. To deny Ra, you deny life and all that is good. Some people don't see that. In fact, some people say we're going to fully evolve from monkeys. Can you believe that?" As he laughed his congregation chuckled in unison. "I say, we still look them, a lot of us are hunched over, hairy and with sloping brows. Do you see any upright, hairless humans? No. I am what I am."

In the background many men hid. Some sat on stumps, struggling with their heavy wooden shoes and animal skull helmets. Others stood up, eagerly listening to the generals' commands. Oog was one of the ones who sat but he wasn't fiddling with his shoes. Instead he seemed to be somberly stuck inside his own head. One of the generals, a stout man dressed in robes that blended into the color of the sand, droned on. "Men, we find ourselves in the midst of a campaign. The other tribe has made their move. Remember, this is to free their area. We want to promote democracy and peace. They are nothing but barbarians."

All of the soldiers lagged about, some with their heads drooping. "Come on men! They are the enemy! It is our duty, with pride in our tribe, to bring the offensive to them! We have been threatened and we must defend ourselves, standing for our ideals! Come on!" Now he was barking at them, walking to and fro. A few of the soldiers' attention perked up. Most just silently soaked in the words.

At the other end of the plateau the opposing tribe was gathered. They huddled together in a loose circle, some chatting with others, a few waiting for their leaders' speeches with trepidation. "Gentlemen, gentlemen, pay attention. I'm going to make this short and sweet. They are the enemy. They stand for oppression and fascism, and we cannot tolerate this. They are evil incarnate. Remember, you are doing our tribe a duty. You will be a hero to your people. Now go, go, go!"

Both tribes marched out onto the field. As they caught sight of each other, their pace increased. They each raised their shields and flung their spears at one another. Some made contact, some didn't. Once they were in close proximity to each other, they began ripping and tearing at each other. They dove at the enemy with fists and teeth bared. In the span of an hour most of them were dead and the survivors were badly wounded.

Then the two generals stepped onto the field. "Ah, how have you been."

"Good. You?"

"Alright. Want to catch up and get some water by the stream?"

As the two walked, the first general spoke. "You know who I really don't like? That tribe that's supposed to be on the other continent. I've heard they're real assholes."

Boog stood to the edge of the concrete stage and looked on through his oversized, bug-eyed (and bug-made) sunglasses. His leopard-skin tunic was artfully torn in select places and his wool trousers were skin-tight. "And here arrives Krug Daniel. He has a pretty new beau at his side!" Boog announces into a tube. The string attached to a mile away booms his voice announcing the celebrity news. The group gathered by the fire lets out gasps. They've all heard about his dramatic turn in re-enacting last year's big lion hunt. "Krug showed a vulnerable range that he hadn't previously displayed before in re-enactments," read one review, "and the special effects with the shadow hand puppets looked smooth."

"Krug, Krug, can we have a word with you?" Boog asked.

Krug and his date jumped off their luxury elephant, which cost many more pieces of bark than most people, and wandered over to meet Boog, dragging his knuckles around the ground. "Hi, how are you?" Krug said.

"Fine. Are you excited for tonight's awards ceremony?" Boog asked him.

"Very much so. The competition is fierce but I hope I can take home the golden rock."

"I see you're going back to the bone-in-nose look. That's been a surging fashion trend lately."

"Yeah. I was feeling a little retro tonight," Krug laughs. He walked on.

"Krug was here tonight. We're waiting on other stars tonight. We'll be right back after this commercial break," Boog said, with the advertisement for a fashion store selling the latest loincloths.

A chill suddenly drew through the air. You could hear a few people shudder, as well as shaking shoulders and the chatter of imminent death. Drops of snow dotted the landscape. Everyone looked around. "What's going on?" Boog demanded. Icicles formed around all the surfaces and the temperature immediately dropped. Everyone huddled inside their jackets but it was of no use. The wind picked up and now their feet were trapped in ice. Through the cold, Oog muttered, "You think ridiculous stuff like this will continue on after we're frozen?"

"No way," someone near him said, "people of the future have to be way smarter than this."

Men

We were men, and such we strolled about the land, chests bared out, our gazes squinted forward. Our footsteps saw the ground shake, we crossed the horizon in under an hour, drinking gallons of beer and having sex with dozens of women along the way. Robert began with one of his stories. "I once went into work so hungover, I threw up in the bathroom on my lunch break. That previous night at the new restaurant they just opened I had three energy drinks and vodka. I was done," he laughed.

Curt knocked over a light pole and smashed it into pieces with a baseball bat. "That's nothing. One time I smoked a blunt so big the boat I was in nearly tipped over. By the time I finished it off, I was so high my head literally floated off my body." He skipped over a hill and landed on his feet, causing a slight crack in the ground. "No joke." We smiled and patted him on the back.

"What a lame story," I interjected. "So you got stoned, big deal. One time I was up in this club and I had so many girls, the entire club was dancing with me. At the end of the night the manager transferred ownership of the place over to me." We stopped at a creek, pulled out fishing lures, and cast them into the water.

As we sat we sipped on some beers from the cooler. We gazed into the water, with Chuck finally breaking the silence. "Dude, I remember one time I was camping out in the woods with some friends and this bear came up to us. I not only wrestled him to the ground but I also forced him to give me a few dollars."

We all chuckled at this impressive event. Dave, however, frowned and got up. "That's nothing. Last Saturday I had five girls at one. I met them at a party and we got a hotel room. I was able to bang all five of them at once, all in a line. That's how big I am."

Curt and Chuck snickered and shoved Dave on the shoulder, mocking him about the impossibility of an event. It's common knowledge you can only tap three girls in a line at once, they pointed out. Robert claimed his pole was hard to pull out, most likely due to a shark on the other end. We looked over at the spot where his reel was at and noticed no such tension.

Growing weary of fishing, we walked on and eventually began jogging, making it to Miami in an hour. "Ah, the memories here," I began, "just yesterday I got so angry I slammed the pavement. The whole road was cracked and they had to redirect traffic for a day. I'm surprised they repaired it this fast." The whole group took note of this and looked about at the landscape, complementing the smooth gravel and great repair work.

We walked around for a bit before ducking into a sports bar. We ordered drinks and sat at a table. The interior had a dark, calm ambiance to it, with the smell of cigarettes and the sound of today's popular songs clear. "I got so drunk a year ago that when I threw up all my internal organs spilled out. I had to put them back into my body. Then my vision became so blurry I started seeing things in the fourth dimension. It took me an entire month to recover," Curt said. We all whistled at the thought of getting that smashed. But after all, Curt enjoyed his booze.

Chuck's cell phone started ringing. He checked it and put it back into his pocket. "That's the wife. It's cool, I've got her under control. Once I was able to convince her to not only cook me dinner but cook for the girl I'm cheating on her with. Then I conjured up a small tornado in the front room and yelled at her to clean it up." We applauded the sublime bravado Chuck displayed. He was a cool guy, after all.

In the corner a few girls were gathered, playing pool. With their long hair, hoop earrings, and skimpy wardrobes, we undressed them with our eyes. They saw us and turned their heads. We collectively agreed they were playing hard to get with us. "Damn," Dave commented, "I would tear that ass up. I bet you, I'd had all three of them fighting for me. If they're hookers, they'll give me the money back." We laughed, fist bumped Dave, and continued to get drunker.

After a few hours, we stumbled out the bar. Robert began to slur, "Guys, I've gotten up to benching a ton with just my index finger. When I work out every week in the gym, I try to lift the barbell up with my left eye. I'm so ripped now. I think I might have developed abs on my back."

We ascended to the sky, flying in the air. We saw some sort of protest or something on the ground but ignored it to keep sharing stories. "Fucking liar," Chuck retorted, "going to the gym is for pussies. I try to jog a mile each morning. One time I managed to run across the English Channel itself without even breaking a sweat." Curt and Robert began arguing before we had to pull them apart. We agreed to land on a deserted island in the middle of the ocean.

"I could build a house on this island in a day," I claimed. "Why, I bet I could even develop a neighborhood and be called the mayor of it in under a month," The other guys disagreed with me on this, throwing out good-natured insults. The waves lapped up the shore, gently dispersing the sand in slightly different directions.

With the sun bearing down on us, we swam towards land again. We came to a mountainous region where the land was rocky, jagged, and elevated. "This is nothing to me," Dave bragged. "In fact, I think I'll destroy a rock because I can." He proved so by, in fact, picking up a rock and slamming it to the ground, which resulted in it being smashed in a bunch of different pieces.

"Bullshit," Robert taunted him. "One little sissy rock. I can move an entire boulder." Robert braced himself and charged shoulder first into a gigantic rock, causing it to jostle and finally tumble over, resulting in a gigantic gray dust cloud.

Chuck and I clapped at this testosterone-laden demonstration, periodically turning our heads to one another to share words of being impressed. Dave, however, was not supportive. "Whatever, dude. You're always trying to outdo me and impress these fags. I'm going to lift up a whole mountain and throw it." We told him there was no way he could do it. Not heeding our advice, he cracked his knuckles, got into a squatting position, and went to lift up a whole mountain. As sweat poured down his body, his face turned red, and he let out the most exasperated yelling ever, all his straining paid off. The mountain slowly tore off its foundation, with small pebbles falling to the ground in a veritable storm of them.

With the mountain high above his head, Dave threw his whole body into tossing it. We watched it careen down the horizon, scraping the ground with numerous flips. We patted him on the back and exchanged high-fives. As it sank in, however, I found I was displeased. "Bro, fuck that shit. I'll go into outer space and kick a planet out of order." The other guys gasped and yelled how that was virtually impossible. "Yeah, if you're not badass like I am," I explained. "I knocked a star into another galaxy just a month ago playing football out there."

Venturing out into the cosmos, everybody was curious to see if I could pull this off. I laughed off their doubts, knowing this would be a piece of cake. As we came near Jupiter, I lifted my foot up and with all my energy gave it the hardest kick I could. To the astonishment of my friends, the planet went spiraling out into the blackness of space. A hush fell over the group for a few seconds. Then we all began ribbing Dave. Chuck said Curt only accomplished a "B-grade seismic shift." We all laughed at such a clever insult.

Chuck paced around a bit before we noticed he had something on his mind. "What's up?" Robert asked him,

"You guys are so gay. I'm going to do something to top all of this."

We snickered and looked at each other. "What could you possibly do that will be more awesome?" we asked him.

He stood still for a minute, a smile coming over his face, and then he looked at us with a mischievous grin. "I'm going to tear a hole in the time-space continuum and end the universe."

Now we gasped. "No way, dude," we pleaded with him, "that would be dangerous. Existence as we know would cease to be."

Chuck grabbed a fistful of matter and began tearing away at it. A slight hole opened up, with stars and seconds disappearing as he did so. We rushed over to pull him off but he elbowed us away. All we could do was helplessly watch as he wrecked the universe. With glee he punched holes in space. Soon we and the universe would die. Perhaps manliness

Toward The Kallipolis

We were drifting through the desert, Z and I, just wandering, the wind blowing, the sand moving, the eternal heat of the sun bearing down on us. Z was wearing brown raggedy clothes, thick black boots, his stringy hair and beard obscuring his face. We stumbled up a hill before he collapsed. "Are you okay?" I asked him, bending down by his side.

As he rolled over his cheek was covered in sand. "No. No more," he said, "I can't go on any longer." He lay there, his black eyes seemingly lost in the horizon of the sky. Without hesitation he then sat up. "Let's go," he announced as we set off.

I'm not sure how long I've been traveling with Z through the desert. It could be days, weeks, months, years. As we travel through this arid abyss my thoughts drift: to memories of childhood, attempting to ride on my dog, playing on the sidewalk with my toy cars, laughing as my mother bathed me. Out here there is no time, time has stopped, time is looping on itself. An eye has grown on my forehead and I realize this "I" I am is you and I am simply a projection and magnification of your (and by extension the collective) consciousness. Z pays no attention as I say this, trying to push the dog inside his tote back back into its leathery quarter.

Since we are tired, we stop by a lake and crouch, cupping the water in our hands and lapping at our faces with it. Z pauses and stares into the water. As he seemingly ponders something, a hand breaks through the surface and grabs Z by the collar. He screams in terror as the strong, pale arm attempts to drag him under the surface. It succeeds, pulling Z into the water. I jump in after him. Underwater, it is completely clear. The rocks and land give way to a city, a sort of Atlantis. The hand that took Z belongs to a naked man with medium-length brown hair. Z punches the man in the face and swims back up to the surface.

We are looking for something, Z and I. We have been searching for it our whole lives. In our heads, the back of our minds, we chase after it. We run down roads and travel through back alleys. Once, in my twenties, I dug through a trash can for a whole hour looking for it. Our journey has taken us to the desert. It is said to be solid, concrete, physical. Supposedly there are a couple of them. We have been following it our whole lives. These forms, these shapes, these things, we long to look at them, hold them in our hands, cradle them.

We're not even sure if we can travel down this particular path since it is winding and curving. We stumble with the direction of the road, occasionally bumping into each other. The sky drops down, right near our heads, and we can feel the air around us tighten. We barely soldier on, struggling to place on foot in front of the other. Our breathing is labored. Z becomes pissed off at this and tackles me. I lay on the ground, struggling from side to side as he smacks me about my body. I push him off and we fight.
He pulls out a sword and slashes me across my arms. I retrieve a chainsaw from my backpack and disembowel him. He slashes my throat. We lie in front of each other, dismembered, mortally hemorrhaging, exhausted, out of breath, staring at each other in silent hatred. In a minute we are reborn.

A decade passes and we stop at an abandoned gas station, a bit weary of trudging on. We elect to take a break for awhile, setting down our belongings. We drop our tires, hats, and a box of dead mice we've recently began carrying with us. My umbrella makes a thud as I drop it to the ground. Underneath the shade, next to a pump, an old man sits. He wears a beaten-up blue flannel shirt and a diaper. There are crumbs in his beard and his unkempt gray hair sways with the wind. He munches on a sandwich. "Hey," I say to him.

He glances up, still sitting on the ground in the lotus position. "Hello," he answers back. "What are you doing here?" he asks.

"Just sitting here," I say. Z and I look at each other. "Why?" I inquire.

"Eating my sandwich, man."

"That's it?" Z prods him further.

"That's it." He takes a slow, careful bite. "That's all you need."

We think about it. As we step away we feel a tangible change around us. Glancing back, we see visible undulations in the air. The calm geezer with the sandwich has disappeared.

Centuries are going by, the whole entirety of space is swirling, launching ahead in front of us. Our skin is cracked and weathered. A couple of Z's teeth have fallen out. My eyes are heavy with insomnia and my bones feel numb. I limp to a halt, retrieving a flask from my knapsack and drink it, exhausted with thirst. Z hunches over next to me, the labored panting pace of his breath heavy on my face. In front of us drops a vault. It is colossal and the shadow it casts nearly obscures our vision.

We walk up to it, curious as to where it came from or what its purpose is. I touch it; its black surface is smooth and cold. Z walks around the edge of it, eyeing it carefully. A door opens up at the top and a stern-looking man in a military uniform with a ruddy complexion came out. He stands at attention, staring straight ahead with his arms folded behind his back. "This is here for you. This has always been here for you," he sternly announces. Several barbarians in suits rush out and begin attacking us, holding us to the ground as they do so.

In the middle of the desert there is a ladder. It stretches up into the sky, although where it leads to no one really knows. It is the stuff of lore and apparently many are afraid to cross it. Me and Z encountered it the other day. It is a plain silver ladder, with thin rungs that are evenly spaced apart from each other. I glance upwards; it seems to extend into infinity. "Shall we climb it?" Z dares me, extending his arm forward in a playful manner, with an air of smug defiance.

"I don't know. It doesn't look safe," I respond, shaking the ladder.

"Oh, come on. Take a risk every once in awhile," he says as he darts up the ladder.

His foot is already above my forehead before I have time to think. "Z, wait," I call after him, but he continues ascending and leaping up like a cheetah. I sigh and begin climbing as well. With delicate balance I maneuver my hands and feet to continue climbing the ladder. Z is now directly above me. Sweat obfuscates my brow; Z looks down at me and laughs. The wind blows and we keep going. Z is practically racing up the ladder; I struggle and my legs begin buckling.

After a while I look down and see we are several thousand feet in the air. I am a bit nervous since I have a fear of heights. Z giggles, with a grin on his face, and seems to easily scale this monstrosity. At last we pass the clouds, willowy wisps of white gas surrounding us, and come to the end of the ladder. Z hops on the surface; I have to be helped up by him. When I get to my feet I see the surface we are standing on is black nothingness. In front of me is a completely blank void. It engulfs us, swallows us.

"What is this?" I call out to Z, petrified.

"This is the void. We must cross it to get to the other side," he says in a serious monotone voice now, staring point-blank into my eyes.

"But...I'm scared."

"Well, you want to get to the other side, don't you?" he asks. He backs up a few steps, gaining a look of determination on his face. Just as he is about to run, I grab his shoulder and stop him.

"Z, wait!" He glances back at me. "What if we don't make it?" I caution him.

He wrinkles his brow at me. "You have to seek to be the best possible person that you can be," he declares. With that he leaps over to the other side.

As I see him standing there, on the edge, smiling, I gain a rush of confidence and figure I can do it as well. I charge forward and jump. I feel myself falling. In my slow descent I look up and see Z, practically a million miles away, just standing there and shaking his head. I consider myself falling forever, drowning in this dark hole.

As we trek through the desert, grazing through lines in the sand, with no end in sight, we continue searching for the forms. We started this journey and so we shall not cease it. Trudging on, Z mumbles something. "Huh?" I lean in and ask him. Without hesitation he punches me in the face. He kicks at my fallen body as I crawl into a fetal position to cover from the blows. Z stops and walks away. When I pick my head up I see he is far off into the distance.

With Z gone, I wander about alone. The loneliness aches and I wonder where he is sometimes.

I'm not sure why he left. He wouldn't say. Every so often I think I spot him standing on a dune but then I realize it's just a mirage. As I contemplate these matters several cacti sprout up around me. The prickles sear my legs. As I run through this sharp forest, blood pouring down my ankles, anvils begin falling from the sky. One catches the side of my head and knocks me to the ground. As I stagger up with my palms faced outward, half-conscious, the sound of thunder rumbles. Lightning strikes the ground around me. Specks of dust shoot into the air, leaving scorched brown spots in their place.

A brick wall has suddenly been erected in front of me. I furiously pound on it with my fists. As my knuckles begin to redden, it finally breaks down. I stumble through the rubble and beat off an oncoming snake with a stick from my bag. Exhausted, I fall down and cry.

Music hits my ears as I sit underneath the shade, resting by a well. Melodic notes of repetition serenade my brain. I look over and wonder where this tune is coming from. Following the sound, I find a guitar lying against a building. I pick it up, feeling its vibrating reverberation. With my fingers I run my skin over its strings, feeling its smoothness. I set it back down and listen as it keeps playing its tune. As I stand and listen the guitar itself expands in size, soon growing as big as a kraken. I am nearly blown away by its wall of sound.

The notes become visible and the song it plays flows out in waves. Intrigued, I climb the guitar and jump off, landing on a musical note. I ride through the tangible rhythm. The music is all around. It surrounds me; I am the sound. We careen through the sky and dart through landscapes. I fly in the sky through the wave of the tempo, enjoying its sonic bliss.

The ground flows in ripples and I feel my mind floating. A plant in front of me morphs shape. The blue of the sky takes on a stronger hue. The clouds seem to move quicker, as if someone put them on fast forward. My brow breaks out in a thick batch of sweat, my body temperature increases, and I feel a rush of panic come over me. As I kneel and feel a lump gather in my throat, all my senses begin to blend together.

I see the gentle whistling of the air, I hear the saloon to my right. My fingers fall off, followed by my hand. My legs deteriorate and my whole body reverses molecularly. The boundaries between me and the outside world break down. I am experiencing the ego death and realize throughout history, throughout the eternity of time and existence, I have always lived. I was the cavemen, I was the Roman Empire, I was the Nazis, I was every good and bad thing that has ever occurred. I was in every corner, I was in every spotlight, I was everywhere and nowhere at once. My body is simply a temporary shell that will eventually peel. I will die and be again; in the shadows, in the fields, in the rivers, in the cities and the cosmos.

Closer and closer I can feel myself, inching ever so nearer to my destination, my journey, the forms. At the end of a long and winding road I see a cave in front of me. It is a large, musty, ominous structure that seems to beckon me. As I approach the front I hear water drip from its hollow interior. I set a foot inside and as I walk lights flash in front of me. I take different turns..here a right, there a left...and find I end up three levels high. I go to a cliff and peer out before me. The whole ground is below me and I have a clear view of the scope of the whole desert.

Walking back inside, I travel for a while before I come to a row of mirrors. Four or five of them show my reflection. As I seem to walk up to the mirrors my reflection seems to move away. I charge and crash through these mirrors. With shards of broken glass stuck in my body I find at the end of this cave a giant monster. It is about twenty feet tall, with no discernible face except for fangs and heavy black eyes. Twisting while horns protrude from its head, it limps toward me, shaggy black fur covering its entire body.

"What are you?" I ask in a somewhat shaky, scared voice.

"I could ask you the same thing," it says in a deep, husky rasp.

We stare into each others' eyes. I reach for my sword but my hand freezes as I grip the handle. The beast leans in, peering into my face, and breathes quite heavily. We stand there for a minute before going our separate ways. I come out of the cave feeling like a different person.

I sit here in the middle of the desert, alone, by myself, on my knees. I think I might be meditating but I'm not sure. It feels like there's a static buzz in my body. In my mind I hear sounds that I know aren't there. When I think it seems like I am talking and when words leave my mouth it feels like they haven't at all. The ground I sit on seems to be eternally falling, with different depressions all around me. I experience it all at once, all conversations, all activities. The sand in front of me seems to be twisting and curving as it blows. A few dogs form near me and play with each other. I keep sitting and pondering these matters.

The winds bear down on my face and I feel the heat lash my skin. My hair is soaked with sweat and now my breathing is labored. On the other side I can see traveling marauders. We meet up in the middle and come to a stop. There is a fair-skinned woman with long, straight brown hair and colorful pink clothing. A few men are with her, all fresh-faced and with short hair. They have an immense amount of luggage with them.

"Hello," she says to me, with breathtaking green eyes, "would you like some water?"

"Yes," I respond, "I would love some water."

She reaches in her suitcase and retrieves a canteen. I lap up the refreshing liquid and look up, smiling at her. We hug as I burst out into tears. Me and all the guys shake hands before we depart on our way.

At last, finally, I have found them, the forms. I wander to the outskirts of the desert and see them in front of me. They look like an abandoned city. I drop to my knees and behold their beauty. There is a house which is slightly decaying, a fountain from which water flows, and a few dilapidated benches. Out here in the desert rests this once-thriving community. I run up and touch the house, one of the forms. It has a slightly moldy smell and the walls have a rough but gooey texture. As the water drops into itself in the puddle I hear the soft sound it makes. The benches, despite being old, are surprisingly sturdy. I sit for a minute in this city, amongst the forms, smiling, finally having caught my breath at last.